Jim Rabe lives near Coulterville, Illinois with his family and a surplus of cats.

This is a work of fiction. Names, characters, businesses, places, events and incidents are either the product of the author's imagination or used in a fictitious manner. Any resemblance to actual persons, living or dead, or actual events is purely coincidental.

The Adventurer's Almanac Presents:

How *Gorak* Got His *Groove Back*

Jim Rabe

The Adventurer's Almanac Presents:

How *Gorak* Got His *Groove Back*

Vanguard Press

VANGUARD PAPERBACK

© Copyright 2023
Jim Rabe

The right of Jim Rabe to be identified as author of
this work has been asserted by them in accordance with the
Copyright, Designs and Patents Act 1988.

All Rights Reserved

No reproduction, copy or transmission of this publication
may be made without written permission.
No paragraph of this publication may be reproduced,
copied or transmitted save with the written permission of the
publisher, or in accordance with the provisions
of the Copyright Act 1956 (as amended).

Any person who commits any unauthorised act in relation to
this publication may be liable to criminal
prosecution and civil claims for damages.

A CIP catalogue record for this title is
available from the British Library.

ISBN 978 1 83794 039 4

*Vanguard Press is an imprint of
Pegasus Elliot Mackenzie Publishers Ltd.*
www.pegasuspublishers.com

First Published in 2023

**Vanguard Press
Sheraton House Castle Park
Cambridge England**

Printed & Bound in Great Britain

To my Nerd Night crew.

Chapter 1

Our tale begins in the fair village of Gunnar's Rest, on the shores of Ricki Lake. The wise, powerful — and extremely wealthy — wizard, Joel, issued a summons to all would-be heroes throughout the Canabeer Territories. The quests were, undoubtedly, incredibly dangerous, the competition was fierce, but the prizes...

The prizes were simply to *die* for.

As noted in *The Adventurer's Almanac* (Chapter 13, *Places to See Before You Ransack Them*), Gunnar's Rest was a reasonably quiet town in those days, famous for its beer made entirely from tree bark and random fish parts, and the ring of stone watchtowers surrounding it. The towers, of course, were less famous for the protection they provided than for the fact that, in a spate of questionable architectural decision-making, the designer made all nine of them suspiciously resemble extremely large, extremely perky boobs. These mighty stone breasts — watchtowers! I mean watchtowers! — allowed guards to shower arrows, burning oil, boiling oil, lukewarm oil, rocks, the contents of chamber-pots, yet more rocks, still more oil, and bits of furniture upon many a distracted barbarian horde. Unfortunately for the guards, the towers and the matching helmets Norm the Armorer had forged for the soldiers of the Watch had led the defenders of Gunnar's Rest to be known as titheads, Mama's boys, and a plethora of other, less pleasant monikers unworthy of repeating.

The titheads, as could only be expected, had become surly from the constant ribbing, and proceeded to take out their frustration on every tourist, tradesman, caravaner, weekender, adventurer, ale enthusiast, realtor and vagabond entering the town. As with any chip a person carries about on their shoulder, there will always be someone inclined to knock it off. And the bigger the chip, the more disposed an irritated hill troll might be to take a swing at it. When that hill troll has already had a long walk into town and is nursing a hangover from a four-day drunk, a shoulder chip makes a very tempting target indeed.

For the uninitiated, an average fully-grown hill troll stands seven feet tall, weighs five hundred pounds, and is capable of lifting most of his or her own body weight. This prodigious strength is coupled with an endurance that human marathon runners can only dream of attaining. In addition to this relatively formidable size and strength, hill trolls have thick hides in varying shades of green, brown or brownish-green, and bony protrusions at their major joints, along their forearms and on the knuckles of each hand. Horns, similar in shape to those of a bighorn ram, but of a composition analogous to those of rhinoceroses, protrude from both left and right sides of a troll's head. Like a rattlesnake's tail, troll horns grow one new ring each year. Depending on the tribe from which the troll descends, the horns may be decorated with bone trinkets, paint, carvings, or capped with iron (if one is a warrior), or precious metals (if one is a clan leader or shaman).

The hill troll with the murderous hangover was not average. He stood eight feet tall and over seven hundred pounds of angry, miserable, alcohol-fueled muscle and sinew was packed onto his heavy-boned frame. Someone with even a passing familiarity with hill trolls (or who has read a copy of *The Adventurer's Almanac*, available at any local library or book merchant!) might have noticed that his left horn had been replaced by a wickedly sharp black iron prosthetic, that his right horn had been capped by an equally keen point of black iron, and that both had been inlaid with gold. From this, the hypothetical observer could have easily deduced that this troll was a warrior, most likely a highly decorated one, given the quality craftsmanship of the horn cap and prosthetic. Of course, even the densest onlookers easily spotted the bands of scar tissue crisscrossing the thick skin, and the immense stone war hammer strapped to the troll's broad, somewhat knobbly back.

The titheads, however, were quite accustomed to dealing with the mostly human and elvish visitors to their town, most of whom were far less than seven hundred pounds. There was that one aristocrat who weighed at least half a ton (as documented in Chapter 367, *Fat Men in Little Coats*), but little of that was muscle, and he hadn't been a hungover hill troll porting a very large hammer. In their complacency, the guards proceeded to frisk, harass, badger, and annoy this new visitor in the same way they pestered every other newcomer, but with somewhat more interesting results.

Gravity is a bit of a harsh mistress at times. Without it, everything we set on a table would simply fly off from the inertia imparted to that object by the revolution of the planet. Also, tables would have to be bolted down, or they, too, would go flying off into space. And we wouldn't be able to breathe, because we'd also be drifting in space.

But on the less pleasant side, gravity is why falling down a flight of stairs, or off a cliff, or out of bed generally sucks. It's why flying is so difficult, even for creatures with wings, and why dropping a rock on your toe hurts. It's also the reason that, when the enraged hill troll's frayed nerves finally snapped, the tithead frisking him for the third time didn't end up in space when the furious troll warrior picked him up and hurled him like a sack of dirty laundry, but rather, in a steaming pile of roadapples roughly twenty-three yards away from the guard's post.

As cathartic as that action had been, the very large, very upset troll now found himself surrounded by a flood of guards pouring out of the boobtowers flanking the roadway like fire ants erupting from a kicked hill. A veritable forest of swords and spears blossomed around him, while above, he heard the unmistakable melodious twang of bowstrings drawn taut. Sunlight glinted from the steel of blades and arrowheads. Righteously pissed off though the warrior was, the odds were not in his favor and his death here, against these humans, would serve no purpose. A purposeless death was by far more bereft of honor than surrender.

Raising his shovel-like hands, the hill troll rumbled, "My actions were rash. I, Gorak Stonecrusher, did not come here to fight you."

The guards heaved a rather unprofessional sigh of relief. One of the humans, his breast helmet tipped with pink enamel, sheathed his sword and stepped forward. "Glad to hear that, Gorak," he chuckled. "Welcome to Gunnar's Rest. I'm afraid I have to escort you to jail for assaulting my soldier. I'd appreciate it if you came peaceably."

Gorak nodded, reluctantly setting his mighty hammer down. Fighting the guards, even if he could defeat them, would do nothing to further his quest, nor redeem him in the eyes of his clan. He had made a foolish error, and nearly gotten himself pin cushioned, only five days after becoming an outcast. "On what honor remains to me, human, I will cause you no further trouble."

The soldier wearing the ridiculous hat asked for some rope, and gently bound Gorak's wrists. The troll barely suppressed a laugh. The thin rope would part instantly, should he choose to fight. But clearly this human understood the weight of a troll's honor, that Gorak would no more snap the ropes than he would murder a child, so long as his word bound him.

"You'll spend an hour in jail, Gorak Stonecrusher," the soldier said, as he led his theoretical prisoner to the small building at the base of the right-hand boob. Behind them, a pair of guards struggled to carry the war hammer. "After that, you'll pay a fine, and be free to go."

"That's bullshit!" the horse dung-coated guard cried as he struggled to hold the troll's weapon. "Did you see what he did to me?"

The pink-nippled soldier spitted his underling with a glare any basilisk would envy (Chapter 48, *Creatures Here to Help You Get Stoned*). "Soldier, the correct way to address me is 'Captain', or 'Sir'' or 'Captain McCracken'."

The guard flushed red. "Sorry, Captain. But sir, didn't you see what he did to me?"

The captain of the guard nodded. "Yep. He tossed you into a pile of hossshit, after you started frisking him for the, what, third time? Did your mama drop you on your head too many times, boy? You didn't find any contraband on the first two times, and I seem to recall telling you sorry lot to stop harassing tourists unnecessarily. Now, apologize to the nice hill troll."

At this, the young guard turned purple. "I-I-I'm... I'm sorry I harassed you."

"Good," the captain beamed. "Now, Gorak, do you feel the need to say anything to young Rutger, here?"

Hill trolls, depending on the clan, have several ways of apologizing, based on the severity of the transgression. For minor offenses, such as accidentally bumping into each other, there is the exchange of small pebbles or trinkets. For larger crimes, such as eating another's favored goat, there is the Trial of Blood. The transgressor, using only his thick fingernails, opens a small wound in the palm of his hand or on the back of the forearm, until the wound bleeds freely. The size of the cut is based on the magnitude of the pain inflicted upon the debtor. When the wound closes, the debt is forgiven, and never mentioned again by any party. The Trial of Blood, in the language of the hill trolls, essentially translates to 'sharing of pain'.

Gorak Stonecrusher held up his lightly bound hands and dug one thick fingernail into his left palm. When it began to bleed, he showed the affliction to the smelly guard. "I, Gorak, share the pain I have caused you."

"Uh, thanks?" the crap-clad and utterly baffled guard replied.

"You are welcome, human," Gorak replied as the blood began to clot.

Captain McCracken smiled, and said, "Swell. We're all friends again. Ruther, go clean up. Can't have your smell chasing off the tourists, now." As the guard meandered off in search of water, and hopefully, lots of soap, the captain resumed escorting his captive to the jail. "Never seen the Trial of Blood in person before. There's a certain elegance to it. So, what brings you to Gunnar's Rest?"

The massive troll warrior was flustered for a moment, grasping for an appropriate response. Interacting with humans, with their myriad, often contradictory social standards had never been a part of his training. He'd been taught how to fight and kill humans, which parts were the tastiest, and what sorts of risks they posed to his people, as a warrior must.

Understanding human social rules was a job for *diplomats*.

Refusing to stoop to diplomacy, Gorak simply shrugged his thick, bony shoulders and answered directly and honestly, "I am here to seek employment from the one known as Joel."

McCracken rolled his eyes. "Might've guessed. Ever since Joel put out that call for assistance, every two-bit adventurer in Canabeer's been piling into town. They stay awhile, maybe get Joel's attention, and then they leave again. Most don't ever come back. And if Joel's so great, why does he need someone else to do jobs for him?

"I'm gonna give you a bit of unsolicited advice, Gorak: screw Joel, and whatever cockamamie quest he's cooked up this time. You need a job? Check with the Chamber of Commerce, or with the Jobs Board. Or, if you want to get paid well, come work for the Watch as a guard. Big guy like you, won't be too many folks looking to hassle you. Armor might be costly for someone your size, but it'll be better than the rawhide you're wearing now, and you'll be treated with respect.

"Besides," the captain added with a sly grin as they entered the well-lit jail, "with an arm like yours, our ball team'll absolutely *slaughter* everyone else in our league!"

Gorak was, again, unsure of the correct response. "I am honored by your offer, Captain…"

"McCracken. Phil McCracken."

"Captain McCracken," Gorak repeated. "But I must decline at this time. I traveled here to fulfill the quest of this Joel, and my honor will not be satisfied until I have done so, or died in the attempt. After this task is complete, I will consider your generous offer." After a moment's consideration, the troll added, "This is not intended as an insult, human."

McCracken nodded. "No offense taken. Offer'll be open for a while. Just... Don't trust Joel. He's a slimy bastard, even for a mage." The captain opened the largest cell and removed the flimsy rope from the troll's tree-trunk wrists. "Appreciate the talk, Gorak. You hungry or thirsty?"

"No," Gorak replied, stepping placidly into the cell. He eased himself gently to the stone floor and regarded the human skeptically. "Are humans always this kind to prisoners?"

The guard captain shook his head. "Nope. But I've been longing to hurl Rutger's spoiled, ill-tempered ass into a pile of hossshit for weeks. He's been told, repeatedly, not to be such a pain in the ass to visitors, but his daddy's the mayor, so I can't just fire the little turd. I'm hoping he learns a lesson from this." McCracken turned to leave, and said, "One more thing: I don't know what Joel's up to, but if he brings any shit down on my town, I'll personally rip his head off and shove it up his ass. Same goes for anyone working for him. If his jobs for you are going to endanger innocent people, I want to know about it. Can you do that for me?"

Gorak snorted. "I am no spy."

"Ain't asking for you to be one. I just want to know if the innocent people under my protection are in any more danger than usual. If Joel's placing them at risk, don't you think I have the right to know?"

"I will not risk the lives of the innocent," the troll grumbled. His headache was beginning to return. "And I will not accept any quest which does. Harming the innocent would be dishonorable. But I am a warrior. I cannot spy for you."

McCracken nodded, as if expecting this response. Seating himself behind a wooden desk, he leaned back and propped his feet up. "That's fair. Your vow not to bring harm to the fair folk of my town is good enough for me. In an hour, you're free to go. I'd suggest you sleep off that hangover, friend. I'm sure as the Nine Blue Hells gonna."

Gorak recognized sage wisdom when he heard it.

Chapter 2

"*Wizardin* ain't easy," Al Ucard muttered to himself as the infamous teat towers of Gunnar's Rest hove into view above the trees. His feet were sore and blistered on top of other blisters from his long, less-than-leisurely stroll from Riverport. Conventional wisdom said Riverport was a nine-day walk from Gunnar's Rest. Al had made it in four, mostly to flee a very displeased innkeeper with a comely daughter and a penchant for arbalests, who Al happened to owe a fair amount of money for room, board, and bar tabs.

"Was it my fault the spell to turn lead into gold was only an illusion? Or that the shiny, gold-looking lead only stayed shiny for a few hours? Or that his daughter came up pregnant?" the exhausted mage grumped. "Well, maybe that last one, but who wouldn't have gone after that girl? For a girl with a clubfoot, she was so… *athletic*." The mage shook his head. "Nope. Definitely not my fault. The bar tab might be my fault, but I'm good for it, right? I just need one good job, and I can pay off all my debts to that guy. And hopefully, to the innkeeper in Inverness. And to the one in… Wow. I owe a lot of money. As of today, I'm never going to gamble again. I'll drink, and I may, occasionally, smoke a bit of weed, but I'll lay off the gambling. Unless it's a sure thing. It's not gambling if it's a sure thing, right?"

Al had once been a fairly proficient student at one of the better schools in the Canabeer Territories. Then, one night, he'd discovered the thrill of gambling on, well, *everything*. There was a rush, like a shot of firepepper (Chapter 435, *Shit Fire and Save Flints!*) juice dumped directly into his veins every time he won a wager on something as stupid as the number of bristles in a broom. Betting and winning big on battles between squirrels or gladiators kept him awake for days. But when he lost, the only thing that consoled him was the sweet bliss at the bottom of a bottle.

He craved the sweet highs, the bitter lows, and the creamy middles with every ounce of his being. The only time he really felt alive was when he was taking some insane risk, putting everything he had on the line. Soon, gambling consumed time that was meant for studying. Then, it devoured time that was meant for class and tests.

After being bounced from the academy, Al set out to make his fortune the old-fashioned way: swindling rubes. His skill in casting illusions was fairly impressive, considering just how little of his studies he'd actually done. He'd sold diseased and dying horses to customers who saw prized thoroughbreds. He'd sold brittle, poorly made weapons to adventurers who believed the blades to be watered steel. He'd even stooped so low as to sell love potions.

Every time, he'd been discovered and forced to flee. He'd been tarred and feathered at least thirteen times. He'd been beaten more times than he could count. And he'd been thrown into jail so often that he'd learned exactly how to land when the gaoler tossed him in so as to avoid bruising his tender and delicate backside.

Each time he'd been driven out of a town, he'd sworn that the next time would be different. He'd promise himself that he'd quit gambling, drink less, get a real job, and stop fleecing rubes. He'd pay back all of the people he'd cheated, and all the poor souls he owed money, just as soon as he finally hit that big score.

Unfortunately, that big score just never seemed to materialize within his grasp. It'd be so close he could taste it, but dangle just out of his reach. It was like the universe was taunting him. Then, he'd seen the flyer with Joel's summons on it. His big score had finally arrived.

"First thing I'm buying is some new boots," Al told no one in particular. "And a new cloak. Still can't get the stink of tar and goose feathers out of this one."

At a fairly large puddle in the road, the wandering mage stopped to examine his reflection. The last few years had been unkind, and his youthful, angelic visage had developed two wrinkles. *Two!* He was only twenty-four, and he looked like an old man of thirty. He sighed, and prodded gingerly at the bruise around his left eye. The innkeeper had a mean right hook. Luckily, the arbalest bolt had only torn through his cloak, and not through his spine or something.

His hair was growing back nicely. After being tarred and feathered, it was easiest to just shave it all off. Like his goatee, the hair was lustrous and dark brown, kept neatly trimmed with the scissors in his pack — which, come to think of it, were still back at the inn in Riverport. "Damn. I liked those scissors."

Shaking off this annoyance, the mage continued his trek toward the town ahead. He'd gone perhaps thirty feet when the sole of his left shoe decided it had traveled far enough. Al halted once more and glared balefully at his treacherous footwear. "There's a fine portent," Al grunted. "I've gone and lost my soul."

Frustrated, footsore and famished, Al kept walking, leaving his wandering sole behind.

The guards at the entrance to Gunnar's Rest were harassing a very large troll when Al Ucard arrived. A skilled reader of moods, the mage quickly ascertained the precarious position in which one of the dimwitted titheads had placed himself. That, Al noted, was not only an oversized hill troll, it was one of the warriors, and the mighty stone hammer strapped to its back had seen some heavy use. Wisely, Al hung back, preparing to enjoy the show.

It happened quicker than even Al had expected. The troll let out a roar and hefted the guard like a small sack of feathers. And the throw! The mage had studied troll physiology a bit at the academy, and recalled the descriptions of their prodigious strength, but the guard had soared like a fire eagle... before crash-landing directly in a pile of horse droppings. Al, along with most of the other travelers — and several of the guards — had a good laugh.

Then, the scene had turned serious. The troll was quickly surrounded by dozens of guards on the ground and targeted by dozens more wielding longbows in the breast shaped towers. Al had fully expected the troll to die bloodily, after slaughtering a fair share of the titheads, and he'd taken a few steps backward to avoid the spatter.

Surprisingly, the troll had surrendered. Curious. Al hadn't known trolls were capable of surrender. Or reason. The inferior research books competing with *The Adventurer's Almanac* had described trolls as scarcely more intelligent than the average plow horse. "I may just have to meet that troll," Al muttered, as the giant monster was led away, fettered by a ridiculously small rope. "There's got to be a story there."

Soon enough, it was Al's turn to enter the city. The guards proceeded to frisk the mage, gently caressing Al's body to search for hidden contraband. The mage had no idea what contraband they believed he might have been smuggling, but they were thorough. "A little lower," Al teased. "Yeah, that's the spot! No, wait, the itch moved. To the left."

The guard was not amused. "We got us a jester over here," he snarled to several of his cohorts. "Thinks he's funny."

"I don't think," Al replied, smirking up into the craggy face of the defender. "I know."

The tithead snorted. "I don't think you know, either."

Al Ucard's smirk dried up like a jellyfish on a hot griddle. "Huh. Hadn't expected anyone wearing a hat that ridiculous to be so quick-witted."

"I've had about enough of your mouth, stranger," the guard stated coldly.

A wiser mage would've apologized. Or barring that, kept his fool mouth shut. Then again, a wiser mage would've refrained from antagonizing a guard in the first place, let alone immediately after a hill troll had hurled one of his coworkers several yards.

Al drew upon a small portion of the magic floating through the ether like sinuous clouds. In his mind's eye, he wove one of the simplest illusion spells he'd ever learned. Thrusting his hands to either side of the tithead's helmet, he wiggled his fingers and whispered, "Squirrels! Squirrels everywhere!"

The guard, used to bouncing disgruntled drunks and the occasional vandal, had never faced down a wizard. He had also never been confronted with a horde of fierce, probably demonic squirrels the size of large dogs. Screaming, the enchanted man drew his sword, and defended himself admirably against the illusory vermin attacking him. Satisfied, Al started to enter Gunnar's Rest.

A pointy bit of steel jabbed him firmly in the spine, hard enough to hurt, but not enough to draw blood. "I'd suggest you undo that spell," a gravelly voice advised.

Sighing, Al snapped his fingers. Instantly, the other guard stopped seeing the infernal tree rats and dropped his sword. "He was never in any danger. It was an illusion."

"Which is the only reason my sword ain't sticking out of your navel," the older tithead informed Al. "You're going to spend a little time in our jail, magician. Try anything else, and I swear, by my pretty hat, I will end you."

"I'm a *mage*," Al bristled. "I don't perform for spoiled brats or rich fools."

"Whatever. Right now, there are at least thirty bows aimed at your head. Your tricks might let you get away from me, but I'm willing to bet you can't dodge all of those arrows. Now, walk."

Ridiculous helmet aside, the guard had a point, and not just the one jabbing Al in the spine. Cursing himself for a moron, Al marched to the jail. "What's the bail for sorcery on a guard?" he asked miserably.

Chapter 3

Hester had been chosen at birth to be the village's next shaman. She would someday lead her tribe to glory, after the bones of the current shaman had been laid to rest. But first, she had to prove her mettle, and bring honor and glory to her people and to herself. The test, she knew, was tradition, yet still the very idea angered her. The village *knew* she was their next leader, so what was the point in the test?

How she had raged when the senile old bastard of a shaman had laid that demand upon her. She had nearly called up the fire within her to burn him to ashes. Then, calming herself, she had accepted his 'wisdom'. Traditions were to be honored. No one had ever accepted the mantle of leadership without first proving themselves worthy.

"What would you ask of me?" Hester had said through gritted teeth.

The grizzled ancient man had sighed and shaken his wrinkled head. "It is not what *I* ask, but what the spirits of our ancestors require, child. Everyone must prove their worth."

"I have misspoken," Hester replied. "How may I prove myself worthy to the ancestors?"

Her shaman nodded, as if responding to a question Hester hadn't heard. "Yes. In the days before this village came to be, the first shaman aided the mighty wizard, Joel. I am told he has need of help once more. You will travel to the town of Gunnar's Rest, where Joel now resides, and answer his summons for assistance. You shall leave tonight, with only the Staff of Flameyness to protect you."

"Joel? Odd name for a mage," Hester huffed. "Any idea what he needs?"

The geezer shook his head. "A shaman must never be impatient. The spirits will tell us what we need to know, when we need to know it."

Hester resisted the urge to pummel him into a dry, powdery paste. "I accept your wisdom, shaman. Where may I find the Staff of Flameyness?"

He smiled and led her into his humble cottage. Hester's nose wrinkled with the myriad stenches to be found within the quarters of a very old man. There was the minty reek of some sort of body powder, the vile, nostril-hair singeing odor of his flatulence, and the mingled scents of several different poultices. "Now, where did I put that staff?" he murmured, gazing at the room as though seeing it for the first time. Then, brightening, he hobbled over to his bed, and pulled a knobbly, twisted stick from his bed. "Here it is!" he exclaimed happily, handing it to her. "I usually sleep with it to keep warm at night."

Hester gingerly accepted the stick, vowing to wash it thoroughly later. It was surprisingly warm, almost hot, to the touch. "Uh, won't you get cold without it?"

"Only a little. It is yours now."

She suppressed a grimace as his foul breath wafted over her. "How does it work?"

The shaman shrugged. "It's a staff, Hester. You hit things with it, use it for a walking stick."

Again, she resisted the urge to beat the old man even more senseless than he already was. "I meant the flamey part, elder."

"Oh, right. You know, I can't quite remember," he admitted sheepishly. "I'm sure you'll figure it out. Now, you should prepare for your journey. Gunnar's Rest, and your destiny, are a long walk from here."

That, at least, the old bastard had gotten right. The town of Gunnar's Rest was five days from her village, including a day's walk through the upper reaches of the Forest of Despair. Which, although dangerous, was preferable to slogging through the Forest of Meh, possibly the most boring woods in the entire Canabeer Territories.

As part of the test, Hester was allowed to take only the Staff of Flameyness, simple traveling garb, and a single, unadorned dagger. She would have to forage for her own food, hunt for meat, or catch fish, or she would surely starve. Never had a future shaman of her tribe failed the test, and Hester didn't intend to be the first. No one from the village, not even her own family, was permitted to see her off as she departed under cover of darkness.

The first several miles of her walk were unremarkable, save for the amount of profane curses Hester directed at the shaman, the ancestors, and life in general. After the second hour, however, she completely exhausted her supply of original commentary on the shaman's lineage and grew bored. The path was well-worn, plainly visible in the moonlight, and the night was still. The stars were out, and they were pretty, she supposed, but stars weren't anything new. So far, the quest had been one boring annoyance after another.

By the third hour of her hike, she'd traveled farther from her village than she'd ever bothered to go before. Leaving the village was pointless. There was nothing to see but trees, rocks and more trees. Hester began to seriously contemplate lighting the forest on fire, simply to end the monotony.

Those familiar with the forests and lands in the general vicinity of her village knew that the unsettled lands were anything but mundane. Bears, wolves, enormous wild boars and the dreaded giant possums lurked everywhere. Then there were the snakes. And the hydras. And the rather foul-tempered treants, protectors of the forests. For that matter, as *The Adventurer's Almanac* notes, the seemingly mundane wraithlord (what is commonly and mistakenly referred to as a raccoon) can be a savage foe, capable of killing and eating a full-grown man in a fortnight.

Hester had completely neglected her studies of life outside her village, considering such knowledge beneath a future shaman. She had no clue what horrors awaited her, which was why, when the twelve-foot long, serpentine form slithered into the road and reared up before her, hissing like a teakettle from its two heads, she drew her dagger and sliced off a head with a single, savage strike.

The severed head flopped to the ground, jaws snapping at her ankles. The hydra shuddered, and two additional heads sprouted from the gaping neck hole as the original head lashed out at her. Shrieking, Hester blocked the attack with the staff, the enormous fangs mere inches from her face, and stabbed the head with the dagger. The hydra recoiled momentarily, and the dying head split into yet another pair of heads. Now, four fanged, monstrous faces regarded her coldly. Hester attacked, lashing out with her dagger, using the staff to fend off the serpent's ripostes. Every time she killed one of the heads, two more took its place, as tends to happen with hydras.

According to the experts at *The Adventurer's Almanac* (Chapter 53, *Everyone Likes a Little Head*), hydras cannot be killed by removing the heads. They immediately grow two more for every single decapitation, and in the case of Klameth's hydra, one of the few species of hydras with legs, regenerate any lost appendages at a rate which is so improbable as to boggle the mind. In order to slay one of these deadly beasts, they must be set on fire or impaled through the largest of their three hearts, located directly beneath their sternum. The heavy ribs protecting the hearts are layered with impressive bands of muscle, too thick for anything less than a short sword or spear to penetrate effectively.

Had Hester perused the *Almanac* prior to beginning her travels, she would've known that the only case in which severing the heads of a hydra proved an effective tactic was in the century-old case of Gornoth the Barbarian battling the mighty Klameth's hydra, Multiplex, in the Forest of Meh. Gornoth, unable to light a torch due to a torrential downpour, had continued to cleave heads from the beast until the sheer weight of the multitude of craniums immobilized the creature by breaking all four of its legs, allowing Gornoth to escape. Gornoth, who could only count to twenty-three after removing both of his boots, estimated the number of heads at over twelve billion, but the intrepid researchers of the *Almanac* state that the actual number was probably closer to a hundred and twenty-three, based on the number of skulls later collected at the scene of the battle. Multiplex, it should be noted, was not slain in the fight, and eventually learned to use his many heads as feet. He later devoured the inhabitants of an entire city.

In any case, Hester's dagger was a poor weapon for combating a hydra, a fact she quickly discovered when she managed to plunge her blade into the several-headed beast's ribs. Despite being jammed to the hilt into the scaly hide, the tip of her dagger missed the hearts by nearly three inches. The hydra reared, wrenching her weapon away, and driving her back with a series of strikes from five of its heads. The sixth grasped the large knife in its mouth, withdrew it from the flesh, and spat it into the woods, leaving Hester with only the Staff of Flameyness.

According to Chapter 37 of *The Adventurer's Almanac, Magic Artifacts and Where to Find Them*, the

Staff of Flameyness was one of five such tree branches enchanted and cursed by the gray, and mildly insane, wizard, Torg. Torg's staves used the elements of wind, water, fire and also stone to cast minor offensive spells with varying degrees of efficacy. Like all of Torg's enchanted items, these staves were cursed to bring dire misery when used. The Staff of Flameyness, as the name implies, allows its user to set flammable objects ablaze. The Staff of Breaking Wind summons a fierce gust of air which also smells rather unpleasant. The Staff of Wetness can be used to hose enemies down with a veritable river of tepid, brackish water. The Staff of Stoning causes large rocks to materialize in midair above a target, and plummet with a high-pitched whistling sound when the intended target glances skyward. The effects of the fifth staff remain unknown, though rumors claim that it summons a giant, fire-breathing chicken.

Desperate, Hester swung her staff at the nearest head of the hydra like a woodsman chopping through a recalcitrant log. There was a fleshy *thud* as the enchanted wood connected with the upper jaw. Hester felt a burst of intense heat from the gnarled wood in her white-knuckled grip, and there was a muted flash of orange light in the starlit night. A gout of flame erupted from the snout, as though the hydra had suddenly begun blasting flaming mucus from its nose.

The hydra let out a shriek so loud Hester's ears ached for days following the battle. Then, it frantically began to rub the burning head into the dirt, its other heads hissing madly. The mystic fire, however, was not so easily quenched, and soon the entire appendage was ablaze. It flailed about madly, rolling in the grass, setting the dryer patches on fire as well. Then, the beast retreated, its meal forgotten in the wake of its agony, and it fled into the woods. In moments, the deadfall in the forest began to burn, inadvertently fulfilling Hester's desire to start a forest fire.

Satisfied by her unorthodox victory, she continued her journey, only slightly annoyed by the loss of her dagger. The forest fire raged unchecked, lighting her path, and battling the chill of the night air. Somewhere in the inferno, the hydra died, roasted to death. The other denizens of the forest fled the destruction of their woodsy homes, rampaging through several towns and villages. Torg's curses, as detailed in Chapter 38: *Cursed Items and How to Avoid Them*, were always far more powerful than his beneficial enchantments.

Hester's journey to the town of Gunnar's Rest took five days, during which she caused six forest fires, a prairie fire and three field fires. She inadvertently burned enough trees to build 3,643 homes, destroyed enough grain to feed an entire city for a year, and ruined grazing land for 432 cattle. Torg undoubtedly would have ruptured a spleen laughing at the fruition of his curse, had he not accidentally transmogrified himself into a small, rat-like creature, and been eaten by his own pet lizard 126 years prior to Hester's quest.

She arrived in Gunnar's Rest just in time to watch an enormous monster fling a guard the length of her entire village. She wasn't sure what that large, bright green creature was, but she had no desire to be anywhere near it. A few minutes later, she watched as the guards escorted the thing away in stupidly flimsy bonds. Shortly after that, they led away a scrawny man dressed in ratty clothing. Then, it was her turn to step into the city.

A guard, wearing a helmet shaped like a breast, halted her. "Name, reason for visiting?" he asked, obviously bored.

"Hester," she replied icily. After the long walk, her normally volatile temper was more volcanic than usual. "I've been sent here to respond to Joel's call for assistance. Move aside."

He frowned. "Another one, huh? Hold your arms out to your sides. Have to check for contraband."

The future shaman brought up her staff. "You will not touch me, dog."

The guard sighed. "Just doing my job, miss. You really think I want to deal with this? Same thing, day after day... It's always one angry, smelly traveler after another."

"Did you just call me smelly?" Hester demanded.

"Well, yeah. It's to be expected after you've been on the road without a proper bath for a month or so," he responded with a shrug.

A month? Hester's frayed temper snapped, and faster than the guard could react, she lashed out with the staff.

The enchanted lumber connected squarely with the tit-shaped helmet, causing it to ring like a gong. The guards piled on Hester like a pack of dogs on a three-legged cat, and they hauled her, kicking, screaming, biting and spitting, off to a jail cell.

Chapter 4

According to *The Adventurer's Almanac*, Chapter 13 (*Let's Keep This to Our Elves*), the High Elves of Ka'el are mostly fair-skinned, raven haired, slender and tall by human standards. The majority have piercing blue eyes, and are extremely skilled with bows of various types, though they primarily favor the custom-made composite bows available only from master craftsmen within their region. The primary religion of the region, Ka'elish, is centered around a spiritual connection with plants, particularly trees. High elves can live in excess of three hundred years and tend to view all shorter-lived species as laughably inferior.

Inigo, like most High elves, stood over six feet tall. His thin frame was draped in flowing robes and mail made of the tiny rings for which Ka'el armorers were famous. He wore boots of the highest quality leather, which made his footfalls silent and sure on even the most broken terrain.

Across his back, he wore a recurved composite bow once carried by his ancestors. The weapon was painstakingly crafted from bone, horns and thin bands of elvish spring steel, giving it both power and durability.

Each end of its five-foot breadth was tipped with a vicious blade. It could drive one of the iron-tipped arrows in his quiver through a steel breastplate at nearly a hundred yards and serve as a close quarters weapon as well.

At each hip, Inigo wore a traditional elvish short sword, known as a Kreshma. These weapons were each as long as his forearm, with a blade that curved like one arm of his bow. The blades appeared to ripple as he moved, as the dark bands infused within the watered elvish steel reflected the light. These bands made the metal beautiful, but as the metalsmiths of Ka'el had discovered centuries before, they also made it stronger than any other steel blades in the Canabeer Territories. The hilts and pommels of the weapons had been engraved with purest silver etchings denoting Inigo's lineage and status within his caste.

Like most of his people, Inigo detested humans. They were loud, odd-smelling, often vulgar beings, and Inigo felt their arrogance in assuming that they were the equals of his people a dire insult. He would have utterly refused to be in their presence had he not been ordered by his father and the other elders to travel to the small city of Gunnar's Rest. Inigo saw no reason any of the elders should care what some stinking human wizard wanted, let alone one with a ridiculous name like Joel.

But duty was duty, and an elf — especially not a High Elf — would not shirk his responsibilities, even if he felt the task was stupid. A wizard, particularly one of such fame as to draw the attention of the elders, should not *need* assistance, and Inigo was left to wonder why his elders felt indebted to some lousy human.

The city, as Inigo had expected, stunk like a midden heap. He could, in fact, smell it from over two miles away, even over the myriad scents of the forest. Unwashed humans, rotting garbage, the feces of their beasts of burden, the stink of their liquor stills... Small wonder the humans were so damn stupid; the noxious miasma in which they lived clearly caused brain damage.

Once outside the woods the humans had dubbed the Forest of Despair, the stench became so intense it rocked Inigo to a halt. How could the creatures within that place be alive? How could anything except buzzards and other carrion animals survive the putridity? Could the humans not smell the filth in which they milled about, or were they merely oblivious, and happily wallowing and breeding in it like dung beetles? The elf shuddered. This task would be more odious than he'd assumed...

Nearing the city, Inigo was a bit surprised to notice that the settlement was surrounded by watchtowers which were obviously designed to look like enormous breasts. They were even, he noted, capped by well-proportioned nipples. Was this city ruled by some religion which worshiped a fertility goddess? Although he'd never been to a human city before, let alone within one of their many temples, he had heard that some of them praised gods and goddesses solely dedicated to reproduction — as if humans had any problem with that. *If elves bred like humans, we'd be spilling into the ocean,* Inigo thought bitterly.

Steeling his nerves and his nostrils, he strode up to the nearest watchtower. The guards, he discovered, wore helmets which emulated the mammary theme of their towers. It had to be a religious affectation, Inigo decided. After all, no one could dress up so stupidly without religion being involved.

One of the guards stopped Inigo with a weary smile. "Welcome to Gunnar's Rest," the human with the boob-helm said in the monotone of the terminally bored. "Name, and reason for your visit, please."

Drawing himself up to his full height, Inigo replied, "I am Inigo Stormrunner of Ka'el. I have been dispatched by the elders of my fair homeland to respond to the call for assistance of the wizard, Joel, who resides within your city."

The guard sighed and turned to his companions. "Another adventurer looking for Joel." Regarding Inigo glumly, the human asked, "Any contraband to report?"

Inigo arched one of his thin eyebrows. "Elves do not transport 'contraband', human. I warn you now, your question would normally be taken as a dire offense. Your ignorance will only shield you from the consequences of your insolence once."

"Look, elf, I'm just doing my job, all right?" the human spat. "They tell me to search everyone for contraband, so I do it. It's nothing against you, or your people, or anyone else. They just don't want anyone bringing certain things into the city. No need to be an asshole about it! What is it with the foul-tempered travelers today?"

"What did you call me, human?" the elf demanded coldly.

"I didn't call you anything," the guard replied. "I said, you don't need to be an asshole—"

Faster than the eye could blink, Inigo dropped the guard with a powerful kick to the breastplate, drew a sword, and had its keen tip pressed to the prone guard's throat. "I should kill you for your insolence, insect."

Inconceivably, the guard smirked. Hooking a thumb skywards, he replied, "I would disrecommend that, you pointy-eared dumbass."

"'Disrecommend' is not a word, fool," Inigo snorted, before glancing upward. He heard the unmistakable singing of bowstrings drawn taut. In the tower above him, he counted twenty-three bowmen. In the tower to his left, he counted twenty-four more. Even if all of the humans were blisteringly incompetent, at least a few of those forty-seven arrows would hit him at this range. From their height, the humans could simply dump their quivers over the edge and inflict severe harm upon any attacker.

Chastened a bit, Inigo placed his sword carefully on the ground beside the guard he'd just assaulted. Though they were inferior creatures, he was vastly outnumbered by these humans, and the thought of being killed by them was too much dishonor to bear. He held his hands up in surrender, and the titheads disarmed him, taking surprising care with his weapons and quiver.

"These will be returned to you, in the condition in which they are now, after you've spent a little time in jail," a guard assured Inigo. "Come peacefully, please. We really prefer not to turn travelers into pincushions around here."

"If the jail smells as vile as the rest of your pathetic city, this shall be most unpleasant," Inigo opined.

The guard shrugged. "I've smelled worse jails."

Chapter 5

Gorak's time in the jail cell was nearly over. He had used the time to sleep, until the rag-wearing human who stank of tar had begun to whistle the same irritating tune over and over. Gorak would've gladly pummeled the human to paste if it hadn't meant wrecking the bars in which he was, theoretically, imprisoned. The guard captain had been lenient, however, and the troll saw no reason to allow a minor annoyance to cause further trouble.

Once the human had realized Gorak was awake, he'd tried to get the troll's attention. "Hey, troll! Troll! Tro-o-o-o-oll!"

Finally, Gorak had asked, "What do you want, human?"

"Oh, nice, you can speak! Question: why did you surrender to the guards?"

The troll stared at the human for a moment, before responding, "I saw no honor in dying pointlessly."

This satisfied the nuisance, but only for an instant. "Right. Makes sense. So, what brings you to this craphole?"

Gorak wasn't quite certain what the idiot was asking. "The guards brought me here, human. Did they not also bring you?"

"No, no. I meant, why're you in Gunnar's Rest?"

The troll nodded. "My reasons are my own, human. I do not see any way they concern you. After my time in this small cell has ended, I will enjoy not speaking to you again."

"Hey, that's funny! I didn't know you trolls were funny. I'm Al Ucard, wizard extraordinaire. You can call me Al. Got a name, or should I just keep calling you troll?"

Another mage? "You are persistent, Al, like the itch of a healing wound. I have no desire to speak with you."

Al shrugged. "Fine, fine. I can be quiet. Just thought, maybe, if you weren't busy, you could escort me to meet my buddy, Joel." When the troll's eyes lit up, Al grinned. *Got him.*

Gorak couldn't believe his ears. In her cell, at the opposite end of the jail, Hester couldn't believe hers, either. Partly because they were still ringing a bit from the hydra's screams, but mostly because she doubted a powerful wizard would ever be associated with a rag bag charlatan like this Al. Still, both Gorak and Hester realized that, if this sleaze were telling the truth, and both believed it to be a pretty big *if*, Al knew where to find Joel.

Al was about to continue lying to Gorak when the guards hauled an elf into the jail. This elf was finely dressed in high thread-count robes which gleamed in the light, and a suit of that relatively impenetrable ringmail only the best elvish smiths could manufacture. The fine duds and the fancy weapons told Al immediately that this elf was a High Elf, and probably one from an upper caste at that.

When the elf was relegated to a cell across from the troll, Al resumed spinning his fiction. "Yeah, me and Joel go way back. It's why he sent me a letter, asking me to help him screen applicants."

"Applicants?" Gorak repeated, unfamiliar with the word.

"Yeah. See, when Joel issued his request for help, half the adventurers on this continent responded. There's so many of them, Joel can't figure out which ones to hire, and which ones will just get themselves killed immediately, or betray him, or whatever. So, he asked me to come down and help him sort the sheep from the goats."

"You are, without a doubt, a complete buffoon," the elf stated haughtily. "The notion that a wizard of Joel's repute would ever deal with a pauper of your caste, let alone request your advice, is perhaps the most delusional raving I've ever had the misfortune of hearing."

"You calling me a liar?" Al demanded. "I've turned men into toads for less."

The elf snorted. "Have you? You couldn't turn water into urine without assistance, human. You are embarrassing yourself."

"Eat shit, elf," Al spat. "When I take Gorak, here, to meet Joel, you can just stay here."

"If he follows you, then he's a bigger fool than you are," Inigo chuckled. "I doubt even a troll could possibly be that stupid."

Hester sighed as Al sputtered some more meaningless insults at the elf. Why were men such idiots? The hideous thing the elf called a troll seemed to have more sense than anyone else in this goddess-forsaken armpit of a city. At least it was relatively quiet. The mage had done nothing but flap his gums for an eternity, and Hester was fantasizing about shoving the Staff of Flameyness up his ass at the earliest opportunity…

"Will you two shut your damn mouths?" the guard captain reclining at the desk snarled. "Trying to sleep over here."

"You got it, Cap," Al replied. "I'm really good at being quiet. Yep, been quiet my whole life, so as not to disturb anyone—"

Captain Phil McCracken sat up slightly. "Boy, if I hear one more word pop out of your piehole, I'm gonna shove my boot so far up your ass you'll be able to spitshine it with your ugly little mustache."

Wisely, Al fell silent, turning his attention to a small beetle bumbling about in his cell. McCracken resumed his slanty chair leaning. The seconds ticked by. Hester continued to contemplate murdering the mouthy mage in a variety of unsavory ways. Gorak attempted to meditate. Inigo stood at rigid attention in his cell, the elf equivalent of meditation.

Finally, Captain McCracken decided he'd left his charges to stew in their own juices long enough. "All right, time's up." He proceeded to unlock the cells. "You'll find your belongings on the table by the door. I hope you've enjoyed your stay here in the city jail. Be sure to tell your friends."

"I have no friends," Gorak replied.

The Adventurer's Almanac's helpful dictionary, located at the back of the book, defines a *sarchasm* as the complete lack of recognition that a speaker was, in fact, being sarcastic. Hill trolls tend to be very literal, and therefore, quite prone to falling directly into the chasm between themselves and understanding what a sarcastic comment is supposed to imply. Gorak, it seems, was no exception.

McCracken shrugged. "Remember what I said about the job opening, eh? Safe travels, Gorak."

The massive troll inclined his head slightly in a respectful nod. "I thank you for your generosity, Captain Phil McCracken. Your offer shall not be forgotten." Scooping up his mighty war hammer, Gorak lumbered out into the town of Gunnar's Rest.

The day had worn on during his brief incarceration, and Gorak's stomachs grumbled and growled like two very large bears preparing to fight over a particularly lovely female. Unfortunately, troll currency is usually made of stone, and no human establishments would accept such in payment. The troll meandered toward the large lake around which the town had been built, gazing upon the glorious waterfall which fed it. It was, he supposed, pleasant enough to look at for something that wasn't a weapon or a piece of armor. The lake itself, however, held fish enough to sate his rumbling bellies.

There was a crowd of people gathered near the shores of the lake, all seemingly enraptured by the words of a single man, cloaked in grey homespun cloth. This human stood on a wooden crate with his arms upraised, blathering on about some nonsense. Something about an All-Squirrel, from what Gorak could hear over the roaring of the falls. He had no idea what an 'All-Squirrel' might be, but it sounded edible, so he lingered for a moment.

"My friends," the unwashed man in the gray cloak was saying, "each and every squirrel you see, running and jumping from tree to tree, is connected magically. Squirrels do not breed like common vermin, but spawn, wholly formed, from a single, mystical being. I bring you its tidings, my friends! All hail the All-Squirrel! The All-Squirrel loves every one of you, and would gladly share its wisdom. The only thing it asks is that you stop eating squirrels, for the death of each of our arboreal brethren is painful, and that you occasionally feed its many parts from your bountiful stockpiles of nuts and seeds."

Gorak was utterly baffled. Did this human honestly believe that some magical squirrel creature spoke to him, or was this yet another lie? Why were humans so bizarre? Still, if a troll had to choose between a mildly insane human who declared himself a prophet for tree-dwelling rodents and a deceitful, dishonorable wretch, he could do worse than the crazy squirrel-man.

His mood soured by the thought that, perhaps, the prophet of the All-Squirrel was saner than the rest of the small, often pink beings in the city, Gorak plodded toward the lakeshore.

Ricki Lake, as noted in *The Adventurer's Almanac* (Chapter 22, *Water, Water Everywhere*), is the third largest body of water within the Canabeer Territories, and was formed when a caldera erupted. Its sheer size enables it to support a plethora of sportfish, and the lake itself boasts some of the most scenic vistas in Gunnar's Rest. The Vater Falls, a multi-stepped series of cascading waterfalls, for example, attracts hundreds of tourists every year as the Rollinona River pours itself into the lake.

The enormous volume of the lake also makes it a natural home for several species of wader birds, fishing birds and fishing bats. Three caves ringing the northern shore of the lake serve as home to colonies of Jared's fishing bat, a species of flying rodent with wingspans in excess of four feet. Estimates of the size of these colonies exceed fifty thousand members, each of which can produce up to ten pounds of fecal matter each week. Bat guano makes excellent fertilizer and is a key component of the explosive powders utilized in dwarven weaponry and mining operations, providing lucrative business ventures for daring fullers willing to brave the ire of the disease-bearing bats.

Protruding into Ricki Lake is the Whatsup Dock, an enormous stone and wood structure wide enough for wagons to be drawn three abreast. The dock is a favored hangout for fishermen, but can also serve as a dancefloor during celebrations, if the partygoers don't mind the smell, or the bats.

As Gorak approached, he noted the large numbers of fishermen casting their lines from the massive dock, and the dozens of merchants attempting to ply the fishermen with lures of their own. The food smelled delicious, but despite the objections of his stomachs, the troll avoided the crowds, and headed down the beach.

The sand was black, and strewn with volcanic rocks, and its warmth felt good on Gorak's bare feet. Enjoying the sunshine and the walk, he strolled further along, leaving the noise of the city behind. With the trees ringing the lakeshore, he could almost pretend not to see the wall and teat-shaped towers forming the barrier of the city. It was almost as if the rest of the world no longer existed. Right here, right now, it was just Gorak and the lake full of fish waiting to be caught and eaten.

In a small cove, the contented troll strode into the water, scattering the fish. It was surprisingly warm, almost as warm as the black sand. Had Gorak read *The Adventurer's Almanac*, he would've known that the water was heated by volcanic vents in the lake's depths, but although he was literate, he hadn't heard of that marvelous tome of tips, tricks, and knowledge… yet.

When the water was knee-deep, Gorak stopped. He stood very still, waiting for the fish to return. Soon enough, he knew, they would investigate this new addition to their moist world, and their curiosity would be their demise and his dinner. He'd been standing in one spot for nearly twenty minutes, growing bored and irritable, but the fish steadfastly refused to come within striking distance.

"The water's too clear," a gravelly voice informed him. A man stood on the shore, clutching several fishing poles and a net. "The fish can see you, so that trick won't work."

Gorak ignored the man, and slowly drew his war hammer from its sling on his back. With a roar which shook the trees, he swung the mighty weapon, causing a tidal wave nearly six feet tall to race in all directions. His hammer struck the shallow bottom of the cove, shattering a rock into flinders. The fish swam away, completely unscathed by the troll's fury.

The man on shore laughed so hard he was crying. Or maybe it was just lake water. Hard to say for certain, as Gorak's wave had utterly drenched the angler from head to toe. The human set his rods down gently, as one might put an infant into a crib, and waved for the troll to join him.

Sighing, Gorak trudged toward shore, re-slinging his weapon. Crusher of Skulls, his war hammer, was simply not the right tool for the job. Perhaps this human might be willing to share his catch, though Gorak dreaded the price he would undoubtedly have to pay for such help.

The human was dressed in short, lightweight pants, and a blue tunic. His skin was a leathery bronze from untold hours in the sun. His hair was such a light yellow it was nearly white, but his twinkling green eyes were still sharp. Rough hands assembled the peculiar rod, with its spool of thin line. A crank, Gorak noted, extended from one side of the spool. A brightly colored bit of cork was attached to the line just above the gleaming steel hook.

"Do you know how to fish, friend?" the human asked, displaying his small white fangs in a smile. Trolls consider the human custom of smiling to be strange in the extreme, as their teeth are so miniscule and dull. No self-respecting troll would ever show off such tiny fangs.

"Not with your device," the troll admitted.

The angler merely nodded and plucked an insect from the earth near his feet. Gorak watched, grimly fascinated, as the callused fingers impaled the squirming bug upon the hook, concealing the weapon's danger in a beguiling sheath of carapace and delicious orange ooze. With a flick of his wrists, the human sent hook and cork sailing out into the cove, trailing untold yards of thread. The gossamer line floated easily upon the surface of the water, nearly invisible even to the troll's sharp eyes.

Silently, Gorak observed the human as he spun the crank a few turns quickly, bringing the cork closer as the spool pulled in thread. Then, the hands stopped, and twitched the tip of the rod slightly. The cork, and the bait suspended beneath it, bobbed in the water. The angler alternately reeled and twitched, reeled and twitched, until the dying bug neared the spot where Gorak had stood. The fish had regathered, darting through the silt his attack had stirred, eating whatever smallish things fish ate.

Then, quick as a serpent attacking a mouse, one of the fish assaulted the bait. The cork submerged, and the fisherman pulled the rod tip skyward and to his right. The panicked fish ran, pulling line with it. Grinning fiercely for a human, the man laid his thumb alongside the spool, forcing the fish to fight the added resistance. When the fish stopped fleeing, the angler began to turn the crank once more, drawing the fish in. It startled, and swam away again, fighting against the pressure of his thumb. He continued reeling the fish in, and letting it run, until the fish was exhausted.

The angler towed the beast into the shallows and nodded to Gorak. "It's all yours, friend. As I pull it in, come from behind it and catch it with the net."

Gorak picked up the net, enjoying the feel of the smoothly worn wooden handle. He strode into the warm water, dipped the net into the water behind the fish, and deftly scooped it from its wet home. Tired from the fight, the fish halfheartedly flopped in its prison, and Gorak's mouth began to moisten.

The fisherman motioned for Gorak to come closer. He easily popped the hook from the fish's jaw, avoiding the bristly plates that served as teeth. The fish's dorsal fin stood upright and its pectoral fins extended, their spines jabbing at the net in defiance. The mighty forked tail stiffened.

"Go ahead, friend," the angler implored. "That fish is for you. Grab it. I'll get a fire going so you can cook it."

Gorak snorted. "I need no fire, human." He reached into the net, snatching up the fish, and lifted it to his waiting mouth. The first bite tore the creature in half, and the troll chewed bones, scales and meat into a bloody bolus before sending it to his first stomach. The next bite engulfed all that remained, except the tail fin, which Gorak tossed aside. Smacking noisily, he belched several times in the Ritual of Thanks.

The angler smiled, spitted another bug on his hook, and sent the bait back into the lake. "I've never seen anyone do that before, friend. Give me a moment, and I'll catch us some more."

"Why do you share your catch with me?" Gorak inquired, suspicious.

The human smiled. "Because I've fished alone far too often these past several years, friend, and your company is welcome." He hooked another fish, and continued, "The doctor tells me I am dying. A cancer, he says. Bedrest, he says." Toying with the fish, the human snorted. "*I* say, I'll be damned if I spend the last month or two of my life in some bed. I belong out here, friend. I'll fish, and I'll *live*, until I die. But," he sighed, "my wife has been dead many years. My daughter died giving birth to a stillborn son. My son left Gunnar's Rest years ago, and has never returned, and I know not where he is. I am alone."

Gorak was saddened by the words of the dying man. To die of a disease, with no one to strike the final blow, was a fate every troll feared. Such a death was without honor. Hefting the net, he strode into the water, and scooped the fish out. "What is your name, human?"

"Jeremy," the angler replied softly. "What about yours, troll?"

"I am Gorak Stonecrusher," the troll answered. "I am honored to share your company."

Jeremy smiled. "It's been a long time since anyone fished with me, Gorak. Not since my daughter died. I can show you how, if you'd like."

Trolls, while somewhat menacing in appearance, are every bit as emotional as humans, as noted in *The Adventurer's Almanac*'s extensive Chapter 23: *Trolls Gonna Troll*. In troll societies, elders are revered, and youngsters are often assigned to each elder to learn from their wisdom. For a skilled fisherman, such as Jeremy, to be without family and without students would be unthinkable in troll cultures, as this would constitute an utter waste of knowledge. To cruelly cast aside a dying elder, to withhold the final blow of mercy, would have branded an entire clan as dishonorable in the extreme.

Gorak bowed his head to the dying man. "I would be most pleased, elder, to learn from you. I shall do my best."

Jeremy's smile widened. "Grab a pole, then. I'd suggest the one on the right. It's got a bigger handle, so it'll be easier for you to hold."

As Gorak retrieved the pole, the angler transferred the fish to a basket. The troll returned with the largest of the three poles, which did fit his hand quite well. So well, in fact, that it seemed made for him. Gorak freed the hook from the small metal ring at the midpoint of the pole, caught a beetle as it trundled about his feet, and skewered the insect on the hook. Then, admiring the tool, he came to stand beside Jeremy.

"It is a fine tool," Gorak opined, inspecting the fishing rod. And it was. The base of the pole was capped in brass, so it could be set into the ground. Brass rings studded the pole to guide the line. The spool onto which the thread was reeled was also of finest brass. The pole itself was fashioned from the same springy yet strong wood as a longbow, what the humans called a yew. Leather padding had been wrapped around the pole below the reel, but above the brass endcap, forming a soft, comfortable and durable handle.

"It was my son's, once," Jeremy replied hoarsely. "I made it myself, not long before he left. He needed a bigger pole, since he took after his mother. She was an orc. He wasn't quite as big as you, but his hands were still pretty good-sized."

Gorak was stunned. This human had married an orc? He'd heard of such marriages occurring, of course, but it was rare. "And your daughter?"

"Took after me," he said. "Her son — my grandson — was too big for her to carry. My wife didn't last more than a year after our girl died. You know how orcs are with mourning."

The troll didn't, as he'd never been around orcs. The elders claimed that orcs were distant relatives of trolls and made fierce allies, but that was the end of Gorak's knowledge. Still, Gorak nodded. He'd seen troll mothers mourn the loss of children, refusing to eat or drink, until they joined their offspring in death, or were given the final blow by a husband or father.

"Now," Jeremy continued, brightening considerably, "Draw back the rod, just like this." Gorak imitated the angler's movement, bringing the rod over his right shoulder. "Lay your thumb gently against the reel to keep it from dropping. Then, when you're ready, flick your wrist like this," Jeremy snapped the rod forward, as though cracking a whip. The bait and bobber sailed out over the lake. "Keep your thumb on the spool, or it will throw out too much line. Then, just before your bait hits the water, stop the reel with your thumb." Gorak watched as the thumb pressed against the metal, braking it to a halt. The bait and bobber hit the water a heartbeat later.

"I will try," Gorak announced, a bit nervously. It had been many years since he had been a child at the knee of an elder. He brought the rod forward, flicking it in imitation of his teacher. His pressure on the reel was off, however, and the bobber landed six paces in front of the end of the rod.

Jeremy chuckled. "Not bad for a first try."

"You are being kind," Gorak snorted. "I failed."

The angler laughed. "It hit the water, Gorak. You didn't foul the line, or hook yourself, or hook me. The bait didn't end up in a tree. It's in the water, and look! There's already a fish interested in your bait!"

A savage grin splitting his face, Gorak took note of the fat fish inching toward his lure. He reeled in a bit of line and twitched the rod as Jeremy had done. The fish followed eagerly, snapping at the impaled beetle. The bobber went under, and Jeremy told Gorak to jerk the rod tip upward firmly, to set the hook. Gorak tugged mightily, and the hook and bobber sailed from the water, bouncing off Gorak's leather-clad chest.

"A bit *too* firmly," Jeremy explained patiently. "Setting a hook takes practice. Too gentle, and the fish can escape. Too hard, and you tear it out of the fish's mouth. Try again."

The troll cast out his line once more. This time, the bobber landed several yards further out. Gorak smiled, the warm blanket of pride wrapping itself firmly around him. It was a small success, unworthy of remembrance in the songs and legends of his people, yet this one simple act made him extraordinarily happy. Even receiving Skullcrusher hadn't inspired such joy. Why did trolls not fish?

This time, when a fish attacked his bait, Gorak mimicked Jeremy's motions when he set the hook. The tip of Gorak's rod dipped, and the fish began to dive. The troll used his thumb to slow the line leaving the reel, listening to the thread sing from the strain.

"Lighten up on the pressure," the angler recommended. "Too much, and the line will break. Too little, and the fish won't tire. You have to find the perfect balance."

Gorak's thumb lifted slightly. The spinning spool was heating up his knobby skin, but it was surprisingly pleasant and he again wondered why his people had never taken up fishing like this. Finally, the fish slowed. At Jeremy's suggestion, the troll began to reel in the line, keeping the tip of the rod pointed up and to his right.

The fish ran again, but tired quickly. Little by little, it began to come to Gorak. Soon, he could see it, a great, ugly, gray-skinned monster with tentacles hanging from its distended mouth. Its beady eyes squatted at either side of its wide, flat-topped head. Jeremy dipped the net expertly into the water, scooping the squirming mutant up with a precision Gorak envied.

"What is it?" the troll asked. "It does not look like any fish I've ever seen."

Jeremy chuckled. "That's a type of catfish. Voracious predators and scavengers. They'll eat anything that fits in their mouth. Not surprised you've never seen one. They don't inhabit mountain streams."

"Does it taste better than it looks?"

Again, the angler laughed. "Only if you cook them properly. I'd throw that one back, Gorak. It's a baby."

The troll gazed at the fish, which occupied most of the net, with astonishment. The fish was easily four feet long, and still a baby? "How large do they get?"

"This breed can grow to be a maneater, my friend," Jeremy replied. "Throw it back. Maybe one day someone will catch this fish after it's fully grown."

After removing the hook from the fish's rubbery mouth, Gorak used one thumbnail to inscribe a blessing in the skin on top of the flat head. "Grow large, worthy opponent," Gorak intoned. "Someday, I shall return to battle you again."

As noted in *The Adventurer's Almanac*, trolls tend to be an extremely spiritual people. They are given to inscribing or etching runic blessings on, well, *everything*. In the case of a captured enemy, the troll blessing carved or branded onto their skin is one of prosperity, protection and strength. The literal translation is 'When next we meet, you shall be prepared'. It should be mentioned, of course, that trolls do not normally carve the blessing into the captive's head, and that they do not usually bestow such a blessing on fish.

Rather, the blessing is generally reserved for a worthy foe, one which the trolls wish to face again in honorable combat. In some cases, such boons are bestowed upon the children of a fallen, but honorable enemy, or upon children who took up arms against the trolls, but were considered too young to kill.

Gorak looked up from setting his foe free to see that the human was weeping slightly. "Are you unwell, *rasgul*?" Rasgul, naturally, being the trollish word for a teacher or mentor.

Jeremy wiped his eyes on the sleeve of his blue tunic. "Never mind me, Gorak. My wife used to do the same thing. Guess you trolls and orcs are more similar than I thought."

Indeed, they are. According to the research conducted by the anthropological scholars at *The Adventurer's Almanac*, trolls and orcs were once the same species. During an ice age, the troll-orc ancestors were separated by a glacier, forcing one collection of trorcs to flee high into mountains, and the other to flee further south. The trolls quickly adapted to their new habitat in the hills and steppes, becoming hardier, larger, thicker-skinned and stronger than their southerly counterparts.

"Tell me of her," Gorak implored, as the two men continued to fish.

The old man shook his head. "She was the most incredible woman I've ever known. Strong, smart, loving, kind and beautiful. She was even about the same color as you. A little lighter, as I recall. Hair like the finest black silk. Only woman I ever knew who could carry a horse on her shoulder, and dance so gracefully you couldn't hear her move.

"We met when I was on walkabout. In my family, when we become men, we leave home and explore the world, you see. I was determined to fish where no human had ever fished, to catch fish no human had ever seen. I wound up in orc territory, entirely by accident, after a crocodile bit my oar clean in half. There I was, fighting off a hungry crocodile with half an oar, when a dozen orc warriors rushed to my rescue like green and black lightning. They took me back to their village, laughing about the foolish human battling the crocodile with a stick.

"And there she was, over six feet tall, and the most stunning beauty I'd ever seen. I thought that croc had eaten me, and I'd gone to heaven. But before I could talk to her, one of the orc warriors — her brother, as it turned out — shoved me to my knees on the ground in front of the chieftain.

"The chieftain didn't take too kindly to my intrusion. He liked the way I looked at his daughter even less. When he asked me what I was doing in his land, I stuttered like a moon-brained dolt. Took me three tries to explain to them that I was there to fish. They thought I was perhaps insane, trying to catch fish with a rod and reel. Worse, they thought I was a possible spy. I don't think I need to tell you what happened to spies caught in orc territory."

Gorak snorted. "No, you do not. Their methods for dealing with spies are quite similar to those of my people."

"Right," Jeremy agreed, bringing in another fish. "The chieftain gave me one opportunity to prove I wasn't in cahoots with the humans causing the tribe trouble. One chance, he said. Fail, and I would perish."

"What did they have you do?" Gorak inquired, netting Jeremy's fish.

"Heh. They escorted me to the nearest lake. A warrior was there, spear in hand. I had to out-fish the warrior, to prove that I could actually catch fish with my stick and thread." The old angler grinned, giving Gorak a glimpse of his rasgul as a youth, seeking to prove himself. "I looked straight at the old bastard and told him that his wager wasn't good enough. If I won, I wanted to court his daughter."

Stunned by his mentor's declaration, Gorak dropped the silvery fish. As he struggled to capture the flopping creature, the troll said, "You are fortunate he did not kill you where you stood. Trolls would not have tolerated your insolence."

"The chieftain didn't either. He bashed me in the face with his staff and was about to gut me with his dagger when his daughter intervened. Seems I'd impressed her a bit. She made her father accept my bargain," Jeremy stated proudly. "I piled up fish like cordwood that day. We were betrothed, and I had to learn all of the tribe's customs of marriage.

"The day we were wed, the old bastard exiled us both, with just the clothes on our backs, my skiff and my fishing rod. He held a grudge better than anyone I've ever known. I cost my wife everything she'd ever had, all because I had to run my big mouth. Never forgave myself for that, friend."

The troll's hearts skipped a few beats. "Were your children outcasts as well?"

Jeremy snorted angrily. "Of course. That prick wasn't about to let the half-orc offspring of two exiles anywhere near his precious tribe. The shame and pain nearly killed Luela. I tried to fix things, Gorak. I went back to the edge of their territory and harangued a patrol until they agreed to escort me to see my father-in-law. He was as stubborn and assholish as ever. Wouldn't speak to me, except to tell me to leave, and never to return, that his daughter, and any abominations she produced were dead to him, and dead to the tribe."

His knuckles white from the grip he had on the fishing pole, Jeremy sneered. "I went back one last time, when my wife died. I begged her father to at least let her be buried with her family. He told me his daughter had been dead for years, that nothing I brought would ever despoil their consecrated ground.

"That night, I dragged her coffin to their burial ground. I dug a big damned hole, right next to Luela's mother, and I laid her to rest. I stuck my fishing rod, the one that I'd used to win her heart, in the ground to mark her grave. Last I heard, that pole was still there, and her bastard father is in the dirt next to her. I hope he's burning in Hell."

"He had no choice," Gorak sighed miserably. "She defied her chieftain. His station compelled him to cast her out. No one may openly defy the chieftain and remain a part of the clan."

Jeremy arched an eyebrow and stared at his enormous green companion. "Sounds like you know more about crossing the chief than you care to, friend. Care to share?"

The troll shook his great head. "No, rasgul. I am not ready to speak on such matters. Perhaps, someday, but not today."

Jeremy shrugged, stung by the refusal. "I understand. You don't know me. Not my business."

Aghast at the gaffe, Gorak blurted, "No! You do not understand. I... I do not know how to share this. My exile confounds me, and I do not have the words to explain."

Mollified, the angler said, "I'll be here, when you're ready, my friend. Until then, let's fish."

Chapter 6

Al's day wasn't getting any better. After being released from the jail cell, he'd attempted to strike up a conversation with the wench in the other cell. His crotch still throbbed from her response. The lousy elf had found the wizard's testicular trauma to be hilarious. Of course, the snooty elf bastard had thought it a bit less entertaining when Al puked from the pain, directing the torrent of agony-fueled vomit onto the elf's shiny boots. Getting kicked in the face by an elf wearing barf-coated boots wasn't nearly as much fun as it sounded.

"Flat broke and kicked in the balls," Al groaned as he lay on the ground, cupping his groin with one hand, and his bleeding nose with the other. "Damn, I hope they don't swell this time. What was her problem? I've said it before, man, wizardin' ain't easy."

The guard captain wandered over, clearly resisting the urge to laugh. "You've got quite a way with the ladies."

"It's a gift," Al grumbled. "All I did was ask her if she wanted to get a drink and... stuff."

McCracken chuckled. "Reckon it was the 'stuff' you suggested that drew her ire. Pain's there for a reason, son. Learn from it."

"Yeah, appreciate the advice. Not, you know, a lot, but thanks." Al struggled to stand up, fighting a wave of nausea. He really didn't want to puke on the captain of the titheads. "Gotta ask, Cap, why do you wear those hats? You have any idea how ridiculous you look?"

The captain shrugged. "Comes with the job. We wear what the town provides. Even if it does make us look like we've got breasts on our minds. Then again, a man wearing boots with no soles, clothes stinking from his last tar-and-feathering, covered in his own vomit and clutching a pair of freshly kicked balls should maybe consider being less of an asshole. Might keep your stones from aching as often."

Suitably rebuked, the mage nodded. "You've got a point there, Cap. Other than the pink, nipply one on top of your helmet, I mean.

"Any idea where a wizard might make a quick buck? I'm a bit strapped for cash."

McCracken smiled. "Try the Chamber of Commerce. They're always looking for some down-on-his-luck fool to take care of their dirty work." He pointed at a building with more rosebushes than grass growing on its lawn. "Fair warning: Carolyn's a *bitch*."

Rubbing his face on the inside of his cloak to scrape off the worst of the vomit and blood, Al thanked the guard captain, and staggered toward the rosebushes. A fancy-lettered sign out front announced: 'Gunnar's Rest Chamber of Commerce — Embettering Businesses in Our

Community'. Al sneered. "'Embettering'? That ain't even a word."

He entered the building through the most annoyingly ornate wooden door he'd ever seen, barely resisting the urge to light it on fire, and into a lobby that reminded him of his grandmother's attic. There was artsy crap *everywhere*. The furniture was all as ornate as the door, and the upholstery was smothered under fancy pillows too small to ever be of any use. It instantly gave Al Ucard the creeps.

An old woman with bluish hair sat behind a desk the size of a barge, if a barge was painted up to look like a high-end harlot. The elderly bat's blue hair was done up in the shape of a beehive, and judging by her lemon-sucking expression, the bees weren't all that happy with riding around on the crone's head all day. She wore ludicrous gold-framed glasses, complete with a gold chain around her neck, perched precariously on her eagle-beak snout. A steel gray riding dress wrapped around the biddy's stick-like form like a tarp thrown over a pile of chicken bones.

"May I *help* you?" she asked in the most irritating, high-faluting, nasal voice Al had ever heard. He instantly wanted to punch her repeatedly in the face as she examined his less-than-stellar attire with disdain.

Quelling this urge, he replied, "The guard captain said you might be looking for some help. I assume you're Carolyn?"

The steely eyes rolled so forcefully Al expected them to pop out of her head and bounce across the lobby. "Why does he insist on referring such *unsavory* mendicants to me?"

"I'm not a mendicant," Al objected. "I'm looking for work, not asking for a handout. So, got anything for me?"

She shuddered. "Please stop breathing near me. You smell like an open sewer. I suppose you could handle talking to Braw Ni the woodcutter for me. He's fallen behind on his deliveries, and winter is coming. Convince him to get back to work."

"Right. Talk to a disgruntled guy with an axe," Al mumbled. "I can do that. Any idea where I can find him?"

Again, the eyeroll. As Al was wondering how her orbs remained in her pruny face, she replied, "You'll likely find him in the Boarskull Tavern. He spends most of his time there since his adulterous wife left him. It's a dreadful place, really. I'm sure you'll fit right in."

"Wow," Al snorted. "With representation like that, I bet the proprietor of the Boarskull is happy you're running the Chamber of Commerce."

As Carolyn sputtered in outrage, Al dashed out the door. A crappy job was still a job. "Yep," he muttered. "Wizardin' ain't easy."

He wandered through town, observing the people — especially the women — and generally trying to ignore his sore feet as he trod on the cobblestone streets. What did these people have against grass? He passed by shops selling hats and other clothes, a store that only sold cooking pots, and entered a round intersection. In the middle, surrounded by a jam of wagons and carts, of course, was a fountain. "This is why I hate roundabouts," Al sneered as a tithead attempted to unsnarl the traffic. "No one ever knows how to drive a wagon through them, and they encourage fountains."

Still, even as jaded as Al was, he had to admit that the fountain was magnificent. In its center, over two water-filled terraces, stood a bronze statue of a warrior. He was as wide as he was tall and clad in what appeared to be armor fashioned from crocodile hide. He stood in a serene posture, his hands clasped on the pommel of a double-headed battle axe, which rested at his feet. The warrior's wizened, bearded face was smiling cheerfully down at everyone in town, and the sculptor had even managed to capture the merry twinkling of the old man's eyes. Everything about the warrior was content and peaceful, even the forty pounds of birdshit on his mighty shoulders and protruding belly.

A plaque, also coated in bird crap, on the outer wall of the fountain read: 'On this spot, Gunnar the Jolly, finest warrior in Canabeer, laid down the legendary Fluffy Bunny, his favored axe, and declared his travels at an end'.

"Fluffy Bunny? Who names an axe Fluffy Bunny?" Al demanded of the bird droppings. "Is everyone in this town insane?"

"Only the ones who talk to themselves," a voice like smoky velvet stated.

Al turned to behold a rakish figure, dressed in finely crafted black leather breeches and a silver brocade tunic. A supple, dark blue suede hat with an outlandishly wide brim dipped low over the man's eyes. The gigantic, fluffy white feather in the snakeskin hatband undulated as his pointed mustache and goatee spread in a brilliantly white grin. The stranger affected a long cape of the same blue leather with a red brocaded lining, which swirled about him as he swaggered up to Al. Perfectly smooth and soft blue leather gauntlets covered the man's long-fingered hands and forearms. Matching boots with notched riding soles rose to mid-calf. A longsword rode at his right hip in a black scabbard. A dagger with an unusually wide blade adorned his left hip.

Flipping a gold coin with his right hand, the interloper laughed in Al's face. Even his breath, Al noted angrily, was smooth. The wizard snarled, "Who asked you, asswipe?"

Yawning, the asswipe replied, "You did. Or do you not remember events from mere moments ago?"

"It was a rhetorical question," Al explained sullenly. "Who are you anyway?"

The stranger grinned even wider. Al fully expected his face to split open, but no such luck. "Back home, they call me Nissan. They claim I'm a bit of a rogue."

"A rogue named Nissan?" Al mused. "Why not? What do you want, Nissan?"

The rogue chuckled. "Same as anyone, I think. Fame, wealth, women. You're here to answer Joel's summons, are you not?"

Al's heart skipped a beat. "Uh… No. What's a Joel?"

"Don't play the coy maiden, mage," Nissan sighed, shaking his head. His floppy brim and oversized feather swirled in sympathy. "I have friends in the guards. They say you know Joel."

The mage smirked. "What if I do? What's it to you?"

Nissan looked Al up and down. "You, my friend, clearly need all the help you can get. You need someone to protect you, even from yourself. You need someone who knows the territory, someone with far better, shall we say, *people skills* than you appear to possess. Someone like... me."

Al shook his head. "No bloody way. There's only room for one egotistical, self-centered mule in this jackass festival, pal, and you're looking at him. Piss off."

The insult rolled off Nissan like rain off a well-greased duck. "Suit yourself, mage. Makes no difference to me."

"Bullshit!" the wizard snapped, loudly enough to draw attention. "If that were true, you wouldn't have propositioned me in the first place. I'm no common harlot, to be paid off and forgotten! Does your wife know about us?"

Nissan blanched, and his jaw dropped halfway to the cobblestones. All around them, women were glaring at the rogue in disapproval. Before he could formulate a response, Al slapped him in the face, playing the jilted lover act to the hilt, and dashed away. Al made it roughly a block before he could no longer prevent himself from doubling over with laughter.

"The... the look on his face!" Al blurted, bent over in an alley that reeked of cat piss. "What a loser!"

"That wasn't very funny, mage," Nissan snarled, sword drawn. Its filigreed blade glinted in the sunlight. "You'll take me to Joel, now, or I'll introduce you to Maxima, here."

Al straightened slowly. "How in the Nine Blue Hells did you catch up to me so fast? Wait. You named your sword Maxima? Who gives their sword a dumbass name like that?"

"Keep talking, mage," the rogue spat, stalking forward. The runes on the sword began to glow with a flickering golden light, as though a fire were shining through hammered aurum.

Mesmerized by the blazing filigree, Al forgot how to run. "That's a neat trick," he murmured. "So, you want to meet Joel, huh? All you had to do was ask, you filthy varlet."

Nissan halted. "I was attempting to ask, you imbecile!"

"No, you were attempting to insult me," Al stated. "And doing a craptastic job of it. You want to meet Joel? Fine. I'll take you to him — after we visit another friend at the Boarskull."

Maxima was returned to her sheath. "Very well, magician. Let us see your 'friend'. After that, you *will* take me to Joel."

"Yeah, yeah," Al muttered, summoning up some of the power he'd used on the tithead earlier. He wiggled his fingers at the rogue's head, and whispered, "Unless you're afraid of *squirrels!*"

The rogue arched an eyebrow. "I assure you I am not. Your pathetic illusion won't work on me. Now, if you're quite finished making a fool of yourself, shall we visit your friend, assuming you have any friends, or shall I simply run you through, and leave you to die in this, *ugh*, disgusting alley?"

"Damnit. Wizardin' ain't easy."

Nissan rolled his eyes. "I shall take that as a 'Yes, we shall visit my friend and then see Joel'. Really, how have you survived long enough to wear out those flimsy boots of yours?"

"Blind luck and my charming personality," Al responded, heading back into the street. "So, does everyone where you're from dress like a catamite? *Ow!*" This last was in response to Nissan drawing his sword and smacking Al on the noggin with the flat of the blade. "What the Hell?"

Re-sheathing the weapon, the rogue said, "Insult or attempt to embarrass me again, and I'll not strike you with the blunt portion of my weapon. You will treat me with respect, or you will suffer the consequences."

Rubbing his goose-egging skull, Al grumbled, "Yeah, whatever. Me and my big mouth… Where are you from, anyway?"

"Far from here," Nissan replied tersely.

"Oh, like Inverness, or something?"

"Does it matter?" the rogue demanded. "No. The only matter concerning you at this moment is the meeting with Joel. Now, if you don't mind, I feel the time for pleasantries has passed. Perhaps the next time you consider publicly embarrassing a well-dressed nobleman with blades, you'll remember this moment."

"Seem to recall you starting it," Al griped. "So, you're a noble, huh? Bet that's nice, having money, tailored clothes, a big house…"

"It is not without its charms," Nissan agreed. "Still, it isn't all fun and games, as you might suspect. There are many responsibilities coupled with the titles and the fancy houses."

"Such as?"

"Have you any idea what it takes to command an army? Or negotiate a treaty? Or to hold all of those elaborate balls?"

"I'm sure holding all of those big balls is a heavy and sweaty responsibility," Al smirked. "I'd imagine your arms would get tired pretty quickly, especially if you're holding them for the older noblemen, what with the sagging—*ow*! Would you stop hitting me with that thing?"

"Mage, you are far less clever than you seem to believe you are," Nissan sighed, returning Maxima to its sheath. "As if you are the first commoner to ever think up such a tired joke? Really, you're trying my patience."

Al shrugged. "Do what you're good at, right?" Rubbing his newest head lump, he asked, "So, what's a noble, with his very fine hat, doing in this crappy berg?"

"Again, you have more important concerns. Who is this 'friend' we're meeting at the, I'm assuming it's a tavern?"

"Guy by the name of Braw Ni," Al replied. "He's a woodsman. Poor, so you'll probably hate him. Oh, and he's a bit of a drunk since his wife left him."

As they rounded a bend in the street, Nissan huffed, "That dreadful looking place *must* be the Boarskull."

"What gave it away? Was it the huge pig's skull nailed over the doo-*ooow*!"

The Adventurer's Almanac (Chapter 12: *Alice's Restaurant and Other Places to Eat*) lists the Boarskull Tavern as one of the top three places in the Canabeer Territories in which to catch food poisoning. The building itself is over a century old, and doesn't look a day over two, partially due to the numerous arson attempts by its owners during the unprofitable months. Unfortunately, the tavern's timbers were taken from an especially fire-resistant breed of cypress tree, which tends to smolder rather than burn. The stench of scorched cypress almost overpowers the mingled odors of stale beer, rancid food and the horrors dwelling within its multiple layers of sawdust floor coverings.

On average, the Boarskull is the scene of four drunken brawls each day, and the researchers from the *Almanac*'s *Food and Beverage Guide* admit that this number is conservative. They also advise travelers to avoid drinking anything with less than forty percent alcohol for purchase within the tavern, as the higher alcohol content tends to counteract the plagues found in the food. If you must eat at the Boarskull, our staff highly recommends the barbequed spare ribs, as the taste is well worth the dysentery.

Other than the ribs, the Boarskull's one redeeming feature is the price of its beverages. A vagrant paying only in change swiped from a fountain can easily drink his fill of ale or whiskey. The current owner also accepts livestock and other barter items in exchange for booze.

Undeterred by the fact that the bar smelled worse than it looked — and it looked like someone had tried to burn the place down in the rain — Al strode through the open doorway. The door, he noticed, was lying broken in the street. The sawdust under his feet squished between his toes like very grainy mud, releasing the unmistakable scents of piss and vomit. Before he could sink any farther, he dashed to the bar and took a seat, leaving Nissan standing outside.

The barkeep, a squat, balding man wearing an apron and a pair of badly stained trousers, sidled over to Al like a crab. "What ya have?" he grunted.

"Looking for Braw Ni," Al replied, leaning on the bar, and instantly regretting it. Peeling his sleeves from the improbably sticky surface, he asked, "He in here?"

"Mayhaps," the bartender said, rubbing his forefinger and thumb together. "Can't quite seem to recall."

Digging in his pocket, Al found only lint. Still, this bartender seemed fairly stupid... "Gold might help you remember," Al stated, forcing his will onto the crab-like man and showing him the lint.

"Yes!" the barkeep blurted. "Why, he's right over there!" He pointed toward a darker end of the tavern with one hand and swiped the lint from Al's hand with the other.

"Keep the change," Al muttered, slipping off the stool and back into the sawdust sludge. He strode toward the corner with as much dignity as he could muster and halted before a table.

The hirsute man sitting at the table wore only a pair of cloth pants, much stained and tattered. His entire upper body bulged with muscle and fat. His torso was covered with so much hair his mother must have been a bear. His heavily callused hands gripped a mug of ale as though it were the only thing keeping him from floating away. Beside him, its head half-submerged in the sawdust and filth, was a heavy axe with a thick handle worn smooth from use. The man regarded Al warily, from eyes surrounded by beard and shaggy locks.

"Go away," the hairy woodsman said, his words slurred so badly from drink he was practically speaking in tongues.

"Braw Ni?" Al inquired.

"Go away."

"Wish I could," Al replied. "But I've been asked to talk to you. Town needs wood, man. It needs you."

Braw Ni belched, spattering the table with foam. "Don't care. Go away."

Al sighed. This was going well. "Can't. The town needs you back at work, chopping wood. Can't leave you alone until you're back on your feet."

Braw Ni stood, wobbling only slightly from the drink. He towered over the mage, and Al suppressed the urge to flee. "Do you know what happened to the last asshole that bitch, Carolyn, sent to harass me?"

"Uh, you asked him politely to leave and he did?"

The woodcutter snorted and hooked a thumb at the empty entrance. "I threw him through the door."

"Look, things suck. I get that. Normally, I'd leave you to your misery, but I was hired to do a job," Al explained. "Besides, do you really want everyone to freeze to death this winter?"

"Don't care. None of them gave a damn when my wife left. No one helped me, no one cared. They can all cut their own firewood. Now, how 'bout you leave me to my drink?"

Al shrugged. "Really wish I could, but I need the money from this job. What'll it take to get you back to work? What do you want? What do you need?"

Braw Ni gazed blearily at the mage and sipped his ale. Foam dripping from his facial shrubbery, the lumberjack smiled. "You're the first one to ask me that. It's always 'The town needs firewood, Braw Ni! Everyone's going to freeze to death!' You're the first one to ask me what I want and need."

"And?"

"And the town can still go fuck itself." Braw Ni guffawed mirthlessly. "You, on the other hand, are welcome to stay and drink with me."

Chuckling, Al pulled up a chair and sat with the man. "A beer would be nice. I reckon I can sit a spell."

Standing outside, Nissan watched as the peasant wizard seated himself at the table with the drunken woodsman. Furious with the delay, he stormed into the tavern, promising himself that he'd cut the coin to clean his boots from the mage's penniless hide.

"Get up!" he ordered Al in a tone he normally reserved for the laziest of his family's servants. "We've tarried long enough, you feculent miscreant!"

Braw Ni stared at the rogue as though too drunk to be sure he was actually there. "Who's this stuffed-shirt prick?"

"That's Nissan," Al responded. "He's a prick. Wants me to take him to meet Joel."

"Screw Joel," Braw Ni huffed. "Screw him right in his ear." The woodcutter looked at the rogue and spat, "We're having a drink, prick. You can go screw yourself, too."

Sputtering in outrage, Nissan began to draw his sword. Braw Ni hefted his rather large axe and slammed it on the table hard enough to cause his ale to imitate a geyser. Maxima stayed in her scabbard. The axe remained on the table.

"Why don't you buy us a round?" Al asked Nissan. "I'm fresh out of gold, wouldn't you know?"

"I'll do nothing of the sort, you bastard. You lead me to this sewer, delay my mission to meet Joel, and expect me to buy you and your loathsome drunkard friend liquor? I should slay you where you sit."

"But you won't," Al countered. "Can't take you to meet Joel if I'm dead. Why don't you sit down, and buy us all something to drink?"

The rogue sat, his rage causing his floppy hat to smolder a bit. He would've gladly slain every last piece of human excrement in the tavern if he didn't need the wizard. "I'll sit," he announced. "But the world shall burn ere I buy *you* a drink."

"Fair enough," Al chuckled. He raised a hand to get the bartender's attention. "Hey, bartender! Beer me!"

"Right you are, sir!" the barman called, hurrying to fill a mug. He shambled over to the table, wiped a spot on the table with a filthy rag, and set the frothy beverage before Al. "Will there be anything else?"

"Nah. Thanks, Jeeves." As the barman skittered away, Al sipped the beer, which somehow managed to be sweet and bitter and reek of peat moss all at the same time. "Meh. I've had worse. A lot worse, come to think of it."

"Passes the time, and that's about all," Braw Ni agreed. "Course, you don't buy ale. You just rent it for a while."

"Oh, who needs great thinkers and philosophers, when we have woodcutters to bestow such heady wisdom?" Nissan snarled. "This is pathetic. You should be out doing your job, peasant, instead of sulking here, drinking yourself into a stupor."

Whatever Braw Ni was about to say was interrupted by an enraged roar from the bartender. "Here, now! Where the fuck did my gold go?"

"Uh, time to leave!" Al whispered to Nissan. He stood, drank the remainder of his beer in one long gulp, and started to dash out the door when the barkeep flumped himself over the bar, wielding a very large, very sharp butcher knife. "Crap. Crappity crap. Uh, *squirrels!*" Al bellowed, wiggling his fingers at the bartender.

When the bartender arched an eyebrow, Al realized that he'd pushed his luck too far. Again. He'd run out of juice to cast the illusion magic, having conjured three such spells in a very short period of time. Thinking fast, his mind's eye wove the pattern for an ignition spell he'd learned while still at the academy, useful mostly for lighting candles and campfires. Digging deeply into his reserves, he shoved his will into the spell like a man shoving dirty clothes into a sack, and released it, aiming for one of the battered tables.

He missed. More catastrophically, however, he'd driven entirely too much willpower into a spell that was merely intended to set the disgusting tabletop on fire. His lack of study meant a lack of control, and fire is one element that no one can tame easily. It's also a terribly unforgiving taskmaster. Even with the dearth of finesse and the surplus of power, Al's spell might've been less disastrous, had the floor of the tavern been wooden planks, or, better still, dirt.

As it stood, in his panic Al unleashed the most powerful ignition spell he'd ever conjured, missing the table he'd intended to burn, and striking the floor behind it. The layers of sawdust, fermenting under the surface from years of feces, urine, vomit, peanut shells and booze spills, burst eagerly into flame. The pillar of fire licked the ceiling as it blossomed, devouring everything around it — and completely blocking the only door with a wall of flames.

The windows, by design, were entirely too small to permit patrons to flee. Panicked by the flames and the choking smoke, the barflies dove over the bar, smashing bottles of liquor, and upsetting kegs of beer. The bartender froze, unsure whether to flee the tavern, stab Al repeatedly, or go after the customers currently destroying his inventory. On the other hand, at least he wouldn't have to worry about this month's arson attempt.

Nissan, faced with certain death, hid in a corner and wept like a little girl. Al stood transfixed by the sheer horror of the disaster he'd caused, unable to turn away from the inferno.

Braw Ni, unfazed by the danger, finished drinking his ale in a few relaxed quaffs. He rose to wobbly feet, axe in hand, and strode to the wall furthest from the flames. Unimpressed by the clamor, the smoke, and the flames, he raised his axe and swung it at one of the studs. He quickly fell into a rhythm, chopping through the wall as he would a tree, and soon had created a fairly large hole in the wall. He stepped through into the fresh air, intent on watching the Boarskull burn to the ground.

Then, when no one else followed, Braw Ni staggered back into the bar, and proceeded to hurl everyone out the hole. As the last patron landed in the groaning, coughing pile, he stepped back outside. The tavern, his home away from home, burned brightly, blackening the sky with billowing clouds of smoke.

Strangely, for the first time since his wife had left him, Braw Ni felt alive. He enjoyed watching the fire. More importantly, saving all of the people from the blaze had made him feel like a man again. As people began running with buckets of water to extinguish the inferno and save the surrounding buildings, a spark ignited in Braw Ni's mind: Gunnar's Rest needed a fireguard.

The Adventurer's Almanac, that veritable font of occasionally useful information, notes that Braw Ni the woodcutter went on to establish the Gunnar's Rest Fireguard. This band of volunteers fought fires and rescued victims of the blazes using enormous, horse-drawn vats of water, ladders and axes. Although several major cities in the Canabeer Territories had already developed hand-pumped fire engines by this time, the concept of a fire department had never occurred to anyone in Gunnar's Rest.

Braw Ni's fireguards would go on to save hundreds of lives and countless buildings, all thanks to Al Ucard's incompetence with fire magic and a poorly planned sawdust floor.

"Forgot how much I loved swinging my axe," Braw Ni remarked, admiring the massive hole in the side of the tavern. He stood in a pose Al immediately associated with the fountain statue. All Braw Ni needed was to be bronzed and covered in pigeon shit. "Reckon it's time I went back to work."

"Glad to hear that," Al coughed. "Gotta go!"

The mage and the rogue fled. Behind them, the Boarksull Tavern's roof thatching was ablaze. The barkeep knelt in the street, weeping messily as his livelihood went up in smoke for all the witnesses the insurance adjuster would surely interview later, the butcher knife still clutched in one meaty fist.

Several blocks away, the unlikely duo slowed to a less suspicious pace. "That… could've gone better," Al panted.

Nissan spitted him with a gorgon's stare. "You have a talent for understatement. Do all of your excursions result in someone attempting to stab you and arson?"

Al had to think for a moment. "No, not *all* of them. More than a few of them, but not all. Wow. I've really been involved in a lot of bad situations…"

"Those who do not learn from history," the rogue chided acidly, "are forever doomed to repeat it. That bartender wasn't the first one you've attempted to fool into believing pocket lint was gold."

"No," Al admitted. "But I'll pay them all back one of these days."

Nissan laughed in Al's face. "You're delusional! You'll never repay any of those you've tricked. Serpents don't change their scales."

Unable to argue, Al led the way in silence. He was without the slightest idea of where he was going.

Chapter 7

Once free of the jail cell, Inigo had immediately asked one of the guards where this Joel might be found. The guard, unsure himself, had asked another guard. That guard had directed Inigo toward the northeast side of the town. There was a garden, the tithead had said, with a statue of a Grim Reaper standing watch over the vegetables. On the north side of that garden, Inigo would find Joel's lair.

"'You'll know it when you see it,'" Inigo hissed, repeating the guard's parting words. The elf stood amongst rutabagas and tomatoes in the shadow of Death, facing a ramshackle wooden domicile with peeling white paint. Portions of the roof had fallen in, leaving dark gaps in the slate. The yard was overgrown, and strewn with broken bric-a-brac, much of it completely unrecognizable. Timbers had been nailed haphazardly across all of the visible windows and the door. Everything about the home exuded abandonment and despair, urging onlookers to avert their gaze. Inigo's every instinct informed him that this derelict was empty, that he was wasting his time simply being here.

Following his instinct, he turned away, facing a smaller, more pleasant-looking house to the south. This one was in excellent repair, with fresh paint. Inigo's senses immediately stopped their clamoring. Strange.

He turned slowly to face the abandoned house, and the sense of dread and sadness gradually increased, until his sense were quite certain there was nothing for him within that place. Inigo faced the south slowly, and the negative feelings dissipated. He turned quickly to face the north, and the sense of despondency hit him like a troll's battle club. Inigo's thin lips quirked into a smile. "Clever. I begin to like this Joel."

The elf ambled forth, ignoring the nagging voice in his head telling him to forget about this ugly, run-down abandoned house and go on with his day. The nagging got more insistent as he neared the house. Then, when he was close enough for his elf eyes to detect the true ruse, the artistry involved in faking dilapidation, the voice suddenly fell silent. The door swung open, and the timbers pivoted away on fiendishly concealed hinges. Inigo entered the gloomily lit foyer, and the door and timbers resumed their ruse.

"Yes, welcome," a voice drawled. "You are the first visitor I've had in a few years. I've expected many more adventurers to answer my summons, but no. Just you."

Inigo's pride etched a smile across his face. "I suspect the rest were deceived by your illusion."

"What? Did I forget to turn that off? Small wonder no one showed up. Probably thought I was dead," Joel muttered. The wizard shuffled into the light, his black robes swirling around his feet, giving the impression that he was hovering just above the floor. His graying hair peeked out at weird angles from beneath his tall, stovepipe-shaped hat. Cobwebs adorned the black felt of the hat, but Inigo immediately realized these were not affectations; there were, in fact, a few smallish spiders inhabiting the webs. Their beady eyes glittered like black pearls beneath the caress of the candlelight as they stared at this newcomer.

"My elders have sent me to assist you," Inigo stated, ending his staring contest with the hat-borne arachnids. "Why have you called for help?"

"What? Oh, yes, the summons..." Joel muttered, twirling his long, upside-down-conifer-shaped beard. Inigo was less than surprised to note a few spiders dwelling within the dull gray whiskers. Several of them scattered as the gnarled fingers absentmindedly fiddled with their home. "A century or so ago, I placed a few things of mine into storage in the Cave of R'an D'om. It's southeast of here, across the Jane Plain. Recently, some insolent bandits took to using my storage cave as their hideout. Can you imagine the impertinence?

"Remove them, and recover my things, and you shall be rewarded."

Inigo frowned. Had he traveled all this way to battle a few meager thieves and vagabonds? "What sort of 'things' did you place into storage?"

The wizard cocked his head to consider the question, stroking his mustache. Finally, after an interminably long time, he shrugged. "I can't keep track of what I place in storage, elf. Magical items, most likely. Just kill the bandits and bring back anything that looks important. But don't touch any of it.

"When you get back, I may have some other stuff for you to do."

"As you wish," the elf sighed, silently cursing his elders for fools. Why had they wasted his time with this doddering old coot? Was this some sort of test?

"Yes," he muttered, departing Joel's domicile. "It must be a test. The elders never would have allied themselves with an imbecile such as this Joel is pretending to be."

"Found the mage, I see," Hester snarled, standing in the elf's way. "What's this damned mission that everyone seems to think is so important?"

Inigo chuckled. "Why should I tell you anything, witch?"

Stonily, she replied, "I can't return to my village unless I fulfill this stupid quest. I'm coming with you, whether you like it or not."

"Indeed? And why should I permit you to do so?"

"You wouldn't like me when I'm mad," Hester snapped. "The weird snake-thing with all the extra heads sure as all the Hells didn't."

Inigo was stunned. "You battled a hydra? Impressive. Perhaps you'll be of use after all," he admitted with a shrug. "Very well. Do try to keep up."

The elf began walking toward the southeast gates. The would-be shaman followed in his wake, vowing to herself that she would beat him to death with her Staff of Flameyness. They never noticed the eyes that watched, nor those who followed.

Chapter 8

Featherwillow of the Wee Folk had always dreamed big — even for a sprite. She had fantasized about leaving her family's stump in the Forest of Despair and seeing the world since she had been knee-high to a ladybug. Feather wanted to meet new people, explore new forests, and do new things, but most of all, Feather wanted to be a knight.

Like most of the Wee Folk, her family was never really noticed by any of the bigger races as they tromped about, crushing insects, grass and everything else underfoot. Her father had always claimed that the bigger races were just stupid, and their eyesight often too poor to notice anything smaller than they were, so Feather had never really thought much of the humans, elves, trolls, orcs, or any other bigger creatures she'd seen — until the Great Battle.

The humans, clad in metal skin which shone like the sun, had ridden massive horses as they fought against a much larger group of elves. Thundering through the forest, their horses' hooves destroying everything in their path, the humans had been like gods to the sprite. This metal skin had shed arrows like raindrops, and the elves had been utterly defeated.

Feather hadn't the slightest idea what the humans and elves had been warring over, but the sight of those humans in their metal skin, what they called 'armor', had never been far from her thoughts. The humans and their horses had moved as though they shared a single soul, and their armor had made them invincible. No Wee Folk had ever known such power or recognition, and Feather lusted for that glory like a forest thirsts for the rains.

As soon as she could, she had begun piecing together her own suit of armor, tailored to fit her twelve-inch-tall frame. A polished acorn had been hollowed out and trimmed to serve as her helm. Tiny fish scales, sewn together with spider silk, formed a rudimentary mail. A small tortoise shell had been transformed into a shield by threading small strips of mousehide through the vertebrae. Pieces of crawfish carapace formed a breastplate, vambraces, greaves, a dexterous glove for her right hand, and for her left hand, a mighty gauntlet made from the crawdad's battle claw.

She had hardened sassafras shoots, sharpening them to keen points, to use as lances. A steel needle, swiped from a traveling tailor, served as a sword, after she had put an edge on its side with a pebble. Rose thorns, attached to bits of twig, made dandy daggers. She'd even fashioned a mighty battle axe from a steel arrowhead.

But of all her accomplishments in pursuit of knighthood, she was most proud of training her magnificent steed. Renato stood nearly as tall as Feather. His flanks bulged with muscle beneath thick whitish fur.

His growls and hisses terrified most of her family into flight or hiding. His teeth and claws could easily tear any enemy to shreds. Clad in his polished tortoiseshell armor, complete with a sharpened rose thorn club for his prehensile tail, Renato, her formidable battle opossum, was a force to be reckoned with.

To train for life as a knight, Feather and Renato would race about the forest, often at Renato's top speed of a murderous seven miles per hour, executing turns and maneuvers no human knight on a horse could ever match. She would spear berries and fruit with her lances, and hack through dangling pecans with her sword, all while Renato surged along, galloping like the wind. The daily training soon had the rather odd duo of sprite and jack performing at their peak, Renato obeying her every command. No opossum in the forest dared to wrangle territory from Renato, and no sprite or fairy could outfly or outfight Featherwillow.

Still, this wasn't enough for Feather. Being faster and stronger than the other Wee Folk was all well and good, but it wouldn't garner the fame and glory she sought. None of the bigger races would *care* that she could defeat any other Wee Folk. Nor would they care about Renato's meager holdings of territory and his harem of jills. She needed more than the forest could offer.

Her family, however, would not permit her to leave. Her parents had tolerated her, frankly, weird obsession with human warfare in the hopes that she would outgrow it. Now that she was approaching her childbearing years, they explained, she needed to end this foolishness, settle down, find a mate, and raise a few dozen grandchildren.

As Chapter 49: *Wee Folks and You Folks*, of *The Adventurer's Almanac* details, sprite culture is extremely dedicated to the nuclear family. Sprites live only a decade or so, and often never leave the same twenty to thirty square yards of territory their parents held before them. This branch of the Wee Folk strictly adheres to the wishes and dictates of their elders, in large part because so few of them survive long enough to be considered an elder.

Their small size makes them very susceptible to temperature fluctuations, a prime target for predators, and victims to unintentional destruction by larger races. Entire clans of sprites have been devastated by something as simple as an unexpected frost, the harvesting of a few trees for lumber, or the predations of a midsized snake. As a direct result, sprites breed profligately, often spawning far more children than the bodies of the females can deliver safely, making female elders, and their daughters, subject of much idolization. The daughter of a female elder, needless to say, has her pick of suitors, and her bride price can be ruinously expensive.

Feather, as it happened, was the daughter of one of the oldest living female sprites in the Forest of Despair. Her mother had intended to marry her off to one of the sons of the Ferngully Clan in the Forest of Meh, an extremely wealthy (by Wee Folk standards, at least) family, known for their longevity. Feather's insistence on prancing about the forest on an armored possum was jeopardizing that match, as the Ferngully matriarch was under the impression that Feather was possibly insane.

It was with these factors in mind that Pussywillow, matriarch of the Willow Clan, informed her daughter, in front of their entire extended family, that Feather's dreams of knighthood were at an end. Feather was to immediately remove her ridiculous, and somewhat fishy-smelling, armor and turn Renato loose. She would wed one of the Ferngully boys and raise a family.

Feather, who had always admired her mother, was struggling to fabricate a response, some miraculous string of words to convince her mother to rescind that decree, when an accursed wraithlord stormed into the small clearing around the family stump. Raccoons, though only a deliciously barbeque-able nuisance to humans, are bane to trashbins and Wee Folk. The sprites, too distracted by Feather's well-deserved (in their opinions) ass-chewing, were beset by the enormous furry monster. Most of them were too frightened to do more than squeal or flee, as two of their cousins were mauled.

Renato needed only a nudge from his mistress. The battle possum let out a growling hiss that brought the coon's head up. A weeping sprite dangled from the raccoon's paw by mangled wings, as Feather leveled one of her sassafras lances at the invader's face. The coon opened its mouth to hiss, dropping the bedraggled cousin, an instant before the wooden lance impaled its black nose.

The strike nearly unseated Feather as the lance drove through the soft flesh to hammer at the bone beneath.

Blood spurted and the wraithlord screamed, a high-pitched wail that resounded through the forest. The lance bowed and snapped, sending splinters flying. Adding superficial insult to injury, Renato raked the claws of his left front paw down the coon's flank, whipping it with his tail spikes for good measure. Doubtlessly, this attack left a few welts.

Winded by the impact of her attack, Feather barely had the strength to heft her next lance from its straps on Renato's side. Still, as the battlejack wheeled to continue the assault, the spriteknight's resolve steeled her trembling arm. They charged directly at the coon's right flank. It was preoccupied with digging the length of sassafras from its snout, and never saw the blow coming.

The second lance drove deeply into the side of the invader, piercing hide and slipping between two of the heavy ribs. The tip burrowed deeply into the right lung. The raccoon's cries turned into a gurgle. Feather let the lance go, and prepared to draw her sword, Needle.

Then, Renato plowed into the wounded raccoon with all the momentum his fourteen-pound body could impart. The raccoon, though much heavier, crumpled under the blow, too crippled by pain to counterattack. Feather was hurled from the saddle but managed to get her wings working before striking the ground. She hovered, Needle drawn, as Renato savagely bit and clawed the stricken raccoon. The coon fought gamely, snapping fiercely at the opossum, but Renato's training and armor gave him an unnatural edge.

Stymied by armor its teeth couldn't penetrate, faced by an opossum that was far more aggressive and better at fighting than it should have been (opossums are normally fairly docile creatures, despite their somewhat monstrous appearance), the invader attempted to flee. Renato caught its left rear foot in his mouth. There was a crunch, a blood-frothed shriek from the coon, and it whirled to snap at the possum. Feather dove, and Needle carved a furrow across the raccoon's left flank. When it turned to feebly lash out at Feather, Renato tore into the right hindleg. The coon's rear legs disabled, it again tried to flee. Feather dove once more, driving Needle deeply into its neck. Blood sprayed in heavy gouts, and the raccoon's movements slowed... and stopped.

In the space of moments, Feather and her gallant battlejack, Renato, had defeated the worst foe her clan had faced in years. Her family stood in awe for a few heartbeats, before falling upon the dead raccoon like flying piranha. The beast would feed them for weeks, and Feather had proven herself in combat.

"I will not marry until I am ready, Mother," Feather announced, as she landed before the matriarch of her clan. Hot blood dripped from her armor as she knelt, her sword held in her gore-streaked right hand. "And I will not give up my dreams."

"No," Pussywillow agreed, a bit faint from the sight of two of her nephews being mauled by the raccoon. Their injuries would heal eventually, but without Feather, they would have been carried to the stream to be washed and eaten. "But you shall be no Willow when you marry."

A collective gasp went up from the clan. Was Feather to be exiled for her refusal to obey the matriarch, even after her heroics? Feather's heart stuttered, and she couldn't breathe. She wanted glory, but to lose her family for it?

Pussywillow smiled down at her daughter. "From this day forth, you shall be known as Feather Coonslayer. Your mate, and all of your children, shall be of the Coonslayer Clan."

Her own clan? Feather was to have her own clan, named after her? In all of her wildest dreams, she had never once believed such a thing might be possible. She would be the first sprite in nearly twenty generations of Willows to start a new clan.

"Th-thank you, Mother," Feather Coonslayer sputtered, somehow managing to find that much of her voice. "I'll make you proud."

Pussywillow's smiled widened. "You already have. I was wrong to believe your dreams should be shattered, my daughter, as you have just proven. Go forth, seek your glory. When you are ready, the Willow Clan will assist you in finding your home."

Feather rose on shaking knees. Her right arm ached from the jarring impacts of the lance, and her stomach felt as though she'd eaten an entire swarm of bees. Her armor was in dire need of cleaning, Renato's required repairs, and Needle would have to be sharpened, but she was vindicated. Even without wings she would've flown to ready her things for the next day.

Tomorrow, she would leave the only home she'd ever known.

Chapter 9

Night had fallen in the town of Gunnar's Rest, yet Gorak and his new friend and mentor still fished. The enormous bats which populated the trio of caves around the northern shore of Ricki Lake had come out, and their screeches were beginning to give the troll a headache. Giant rodents with wings made from skin were not a sight common in the Highlands, for which Gorak was becoming increasingly grateful.

"Are those winged rats always this loud?" Gorak asked irritably, reeling in yet another catfish.

Jeremy chuckled. "No. During mating season they're much, much worse. We've caught a decent haul, friend, but we'll need to keep the campfire going, or the damn air rats will poach our fish."

"Vile creatures," Gorak huffed. "Why do you humans not destroy them?"

"They're useful," the angler started to explain. "The young ones eat their weight in mosquitoes and other biting insects, and their excrement is used to make explosive powder, women's makeup and fertilizer."

The troll blinked in mingled shock and horror. "Your females smear the feces of flying rats on their faces? Are they insane?"

"You haven't met many human females, have you?"

"No," Gorak admitted. "I have not. You have a bite, *rasgul*."

Jeremy's pole bent alarmingly under the strain of a heavy strike on his bait. The angler expertly fed the fish line, attempting to wear it down. "May need some help with this one, friend. Feels like a big one."

Gorak quickly settled his latest catfish into the basket and placed his pole to the side. His teacher battled the unseen monster for ages, but it seemed to draw no closer to shore. Then, the fish ran straight at them, attempting to put slack into the line. Jeremy reeled like a madman, scarcely keeping the line taut, and the great fish reared from the water.

It was gigantic, nearly as long as Gorak was tall. Its scales glistened orange in the moonlight as it walked across the surface of the water on its fan-shaped tail. Three huge eyes stared down at the fishermen from their perch above a mouthful of triangular, razor-edged teeth. This was Death, wearing scales and slime in place of its normal robe, and it bore down on Jeremy like a smelly avalanche, intent on devouring him.

As *The Adventurer's Almanac* notes, trolls are fairly quick for their size in short bursts. This intense speed enables them to escape predators, dodge attacks, and in the case of the massive three-eyed fish, remove a weapon from its harness quicker than a lightning strike and smash it into an opponent's face.

Skullcrusher, in this instance, failed to live up to its name. The weapon did, however, deal the monster such a stunning blow that its primitive brain temporarily shut down. The fish lay, quite unconscious, on the beach beside Jeremy. The angler drew a well-honed knife and drove it deeply into the leftmost eye socket, piercing the brain.

"I think that's the biggest fish I've ever caught," Jeremy stated. "You have my thanks, friend. I do believe you saved my life."

Gorak nodded grimly. "The fish was a worthy foe."

"I don't know if I'll ever be able to repay the favor," the dying fisherman said.

"You taught me to fish," the troll responded solemnly. "Consider our scales even."

Jeremy shook his head. "Not yet. You should keep that rod and reel, friend. If my prodigal son ever returns, I can always build him a new one. Now, care to help me carry our haul home? Something tells me we'll be cleaning fish for a while."

Grinning broadly, Gorak hefted the gigantic carcass over his right shoulder, scooped up his shield and the basket of fish with the other, and said, "It would be my pleasure, *rasgul*."

The odd pair hiked into town, stopping a few times to allow Jeremy's weary body to rest. Each time, the old man began apologizing for his failing body. Each time, Gorak interrupted him. The troll's heat vision allowed him to see well at night, but it also enabled him to see the disrupted flow of blood around the cancer. Gorak knew the old man didn't have much time left on this world. Soon, perhaps a matter of days, this kind and lonely human would die.

They were near Jeremy's shop, a low-slung stone building from which he sold his fresh catches and preserved fish, when a trio of brigands stepped into their path. The men were dressed in black, with scarves concealing their faces. Two of them bore longswords, while the third carried an axe.

"Money or your lives," the one with the axe said in a conversational tone, as though merely commenting upon the weather.

Gorak was more than a little surprised. He towered over these imbeciles and could easily crush them. Perhaps they assumed his burdens rendered him helpless, because he couldn't possibly draw his war hammer. A step closer, he decided, and they would see just how 'helpless' a troll could be.

"Don't have any money," Jeremy replied. "Never a tithead about when you actually need one, is there?"

"Doesn't seem to be," the axeman agreed with a nod. "Last chance, old man. We'd prefer to do this the—"

Gorak lunged forward, letting the mighty fish slide from his shoulder. He caught the tail of the monster in his big right hand, bellowed a savage war cry that rattled windows and woke children for blocks, and swung the fish like a moist, scaly club. The fish, which outweighed the first bandit by a good fifty pounds, slammed into him with the force of a battering ram. He flew through the air like a sack of potatoes, leaving his boots behind.

Spinning, the troll bashed the first swordsman with a backhanded strike, sending the human through the wall of a nearby house. The last bandit turned to flee, which only enraged the troll further. Lashing out with his heavy right foot, Gorak drove his heel into the crook's backside. The kick in the ass caused the human to sprawl face-first into the pavement, breaking several teeth. Setting the fish aside, the troll rushed forward, snatching up the pathetic human with his free hand, and preparing to finish him off.

"No, friend," Jeremy soothed. "You've beaten them. There's no need to kill him. Please, put him down. Let's go clean our catch."

Breathing deeply as red crept over his vision, Gorak hesitated. He could hear the human's pounding heart, could smell the fear and the blood, and he wanted, *needed*, to destroy this miserable thief. Still, his *rasgul* had made a simple request, and the troll did not wish to displease his mentor.

"As you wish," Gorak replied. To the brigand, he snarled, "I spare your life only because this man asks for mercy. Trouble him again, outcast, and no hole on this world shall prove deep enough to hide yourself from my wrath."

Dazed, the bandit nodded. Gorak turned him loose, and he fled, crying apologies over his shoulder. The other two stayed down, which the troll found disappointing. He'd hoped at least one of them should prove more of a challenge. The call for battle fading from his blood, Gorak picked up the fish, and they continued on.

Unlocking his shop, Jeremy chuckled. "That was some move, friend. I've never seen anyone use a fish quite like that."

"Trolls are taught that anything may serve as a weapon," Gorak said. "I will admit, however, that none of my people have ever attempted to substitute a fish for a war hammer."

This was not quite true. According to the researchers at *The Adventurer's Almanac*, one of Gorak's ancestors had, in fact, been disarmed in a riverside battle with a very large bear. The bear had managed to knock the warrior off his feet, and the troll, one Targoth Stonecrusher, was inches from having his throat ripped out. Desperate, the troll had grasped blindly for a rock, stick, or anything close at hand. He had, instead, accidentally grabbed a salmon, which he bashed repeatedly into the bear's snout, killing the salmon and the bear.

Of course, no troll worth his salt would ever admit to being caught unawares and disarmed by a bear, so Targoth had simply fibbed slightly, telling his clan that he'd been hunting the bear and had killed it with his trusty warclub. The story, like Targoth's hands, smelled a bit fishy to the rest of the clan, but the bear was delicious, and everyone knew Targoth was getting senile, so no one saw any need to argue.

In any case, Gorak and Jeremy spent most of the rest of the night cleaning fish at Jeremy's cleaning station.

Knives hung by their blades, as if by magic, above a slate table. Lodestones, Jeremy explained, attracted iron and steel, and kept his knives within easy reach. Water, fresh from a nearby spring, gurgled from a set of pipes over the table at the pull of a lever. A bronze drain caught the waste flow, shunting it into the town's sewers. Jeremy scrubbed the slate with salt and a stiff-bristled brush between each fish, ensuring that the station was clean of fish parts and debris.

They saved the giant for last. Jeremy filleted the monster carefully, ensuring that all of the skeleton remained intact. It would, he informed his student, be preserved and mounted to commemorate the occasion, as soon as Braw Ni the woodcutter found Jeremy a large enough tree. The hide, which was also remarkably intact, would be handed over to the local tannery, and turned into a tapestry.

The best cuts of fish were rolled in a mixture of salt and spices and hung in a smoker to cook and cure in much the same way as troll clans preserved their meat. The lesser cuts were placed into a brine of Jeremy's own design. All, he explained, would either be sold to Jeremy's customers or saved for personal consumption. Gorak, of course, would have his pick of the catch.

When the work was done, Jeremy and Gorak washed the knives thoroughly before sharpening the blades with whetstones, readying them for the next time. For Gorak, maintaining the blades was akin to a meditative act and he felt his soul lighten with each stroke against the stone. The fish guts went into a large stone vat, filled with the worms Jeremy used as bait. The table was scrubbed once more with salt and spring water.

The bones went into a large metal hopper in the wall. This hopper, Jeremy informed his new friend, emptied into the baker's shop next door. The bakers would take the bones, grind them into meal, and mix the bonemeal into flour. Bonemeal bread was a staple source of nutrients for many of the poorer families in Gunnar's Rest — provided they didn't mind the fishy taste and smell.

After washing themselves as best they could, Jeremy and Gorak made their way into the fisherman's modest home at the back of the shop. The angler opened a bottle of wine, pouring the maroon vintage into a pair of copper cups. Exhausted, Jeremy slumped into a well-padded chair next to a small fireplace. Gorak, mindful of the destruction his immense bulk could visit upon furniture designed for humans, sat gracefully on the floor. The coals in the fireplace were banked, but not dead, so the troll added a few logs, expertly prodding the blaze back to life.

The two men sat, drinking wine and enjoying the crackling warmth of the hearth. Jeremy was soon asleep, and the troll draped a fine quilted blanket across his host's sleeping form. Even through the thick cloth, he could see the corruption eating away at the human. It was then that Gorak decided that his quest to regain his honor, and his place within his clan, could wait. No elder, especially not a decent one, should die alone.

Leaning against the warm stone of the hearth, the troll watched over the dying man. Inwardly, he cursed the prodigal son for abandoning his father. Then again, considering the rift between Gorak and his own father, his own clan, perhaps he cursed himself as well.

As this dreary thought wrapped itself snugly around his brain like a lice-infested blanket, the troll began to slumber. In his dreams, a stranger cared for his own betrayed and dying father in Gorak's place.

Chapter 10

After burning down the tavern, Al and Nissan had hidden out at Smokey's Inn, a large flophouse on the west side of town. The inn boasted cheap rooms, cheap booze and the best barbeque in Gunnar's Rest — which really wasn't all that impressive considering that its only competition was the Boarskull Tavern. Nissan paid for the night, and the innkeeper's silence, with a shiny gold coin. Much to Al's consternation, the rogue had insisted that they share a room.

While Gorak was waylaying bandits with a giant fish, Al was stretched out on a cold, hard wooden floor watching spiders and centipedes battle over who would crawl into his ears as he slept. Nissan had taken the lumpy, but soft, mattress. The rich asshole was snoring fit to wake the dead, keeping Al awake.

Worse, Nissan was an exceptionally light sleeper. The first and only time Al had attempted to escape, a knife had mysteriously sprouted from the door an inch from Al's ear. The next blade, Nissan warned, would take the ear with it.

Al was faced with one of the worst dilemmas of his short and somewhat shady life. He didn't have the slightest clue where Joel was. He couldn't escape the clearly insane rogue, and Al didn't believe he could best the prick. Fleeing meant death, fighting meant death, and Nissan discovering Al was lying meant death. The mage didn't see a way out, short of finding Joel.

Sitting up slowly, Al drew a symbol on the floor. Infusing it with some of his will, he attempted to detect a strong source of magic within the boundaries of the town. He immediately saw in his mind's eye a few blobs of magical power in Gunnar's Rest, but all of these were tiny compared to the nova of power a true wizard would possess. Still, there was the possibility that Joel had cloaked his power, so Al sent his will to inspect the disturbances.

The first was an adept blacksmith, using his ability to enhance his metalwork. Likely, he never realized he had any magic. Al made a mental note to buy a dagger or two from that guy, as they would be of incredibly fine quality.

The second blip came from some weird fish-monster living in the Rollinona River. Al wasn't sure what the creature was, or why it was inhabiting that particular river, but he wasn't going anywhere near it. A river monster that dealt in magic was going to be deadly, and the thing Al beheld was easily the size of a cow.

The final glop of magicky stuff came from a gazebo next to the magnificent waterfalls. The statue in the middle of the gazebo had been enchanted, but Al couldn't discern the purpose behind its enhancement. It was interesting, but not useful at the moment, so Al drew his consciousness back.

Winded from the exertion, Al leaned back against the wall. He needed a plan, and he needed one fast. What he had was the total absence of a plan and—

"That's it," Al whispered. "Wizard like Joel would conceal his magic, but would he think to camouflage it?"

As mentioned in *The Adventurer's Almanac*, Chapter 22: *Where'd That Rabbit Come From?*, every living thing is suffused with some sort of magic, even if it is incapable of using it. In many cases, dead things (especially Undead) are also veritable founts of mystical energy. Some things, obviously, exude more magical energy than others, but nearly everything carries magic.

Grinning like the fox that just raided the henhouse, Al touched the runes on the floor, and directed his will at searching for *nothing*. Immediately, against the varying shades of blue, he discovered a roughly circular black hole. He almost laughed aloud. Joel's house was less than a block south of the inn.

Spirits buoyed by the fact that he would probably survive another day, Al curled up on the dusty floor, wrapped himself in his tattered cloak, and fell soundly asleep. In the dark space beneath the bed, the spider bested the centipede, winning the right to nestle in the warmth of Al's left ear for the night.

Chapter 11

For Hester, day broke to the sound of arrows striking a target. The stupid elf was practicing with his ridiculously oversized bow. She had to admit that he was a decent shot, but she still wanted to shove the bow up his tight, flexing ass, and why was he naked?

"What in the Hells are you doing?" Hester demanded from her bedroll.

"Practicing," Inigo replied tersely, nocking another arrow. "Talent alone wins no battles. A warrior must train to keep his skills sharp. Do you not find this to be so?"

"I was trying to sleep," she replied angrily as the arrow buried itself in the target's center. "At least put some damn pants on!"

The elf sighed, continuing to plink the target. "I'm beginning to think the hydra killed itself, rather than listening to your constant complaining."

"Keep it up, elf," Hester muttered. "What's for breakfast?"

"I've already eaten," Inigo stated. "The skillet is in the fire, so it should be clean and ready to use."

He continued to shoot arrows in the nude, like a very well-sculpted cupid. Hester tried her best not to be distracted, focusing instead on readying a meal of cured meat and a handful of root vegetables. Still, the elf wasn't displeasing to watch, even if he was a pain in the muscular ass. And as she saw when he retrieved his arrows, he wasn't badly endowed either.

She shook herself. What was she thinking? She was to be a shaman, yet here she was, drooling over some bastard elf she didn't even like. He was rude, abrasive and utterly handsome.

"Damnit," she murmured, willing herself to stop feeling tingly. "This can't be happening. I can't be falling for some stupid elf."

Dressing, Inigo suppressed a laugh. The woman apparently didn't realize that an elf's pointy ears weren't just for show. Knowing that simply seeing his nude body had such an effect on her, the elf decided to torment her as often as possible. He disliked the human immensely, and his parents would disown him if they even thought he had romantic inclinations toward any of the lesser races, but the idea of toying with her seemed like fun.

But there would be adequate time to torture her later. They had many miles to cover before reaching the Cave of R'an D'om. As the human ate, Inigo broke camp. He made sure to bend and stretch in the manner most pleasing to female elven eyes, sure that human females evaluated a potential mate in much the same way. Judging by the human's quickening breath, his attempts to inflame her had been successful.

They walked in silence through the thick grasses of the oddly named Jane Plain. Inigo kept the lush green of the Forest of Despair to his right, using the edge of the vast woods as a guidepost. If Joel's directions had been accurate, the cave would be easy to find.

Insects buzzed and flitted about them as they traveled. Inigo ignored them, focusing his senses on detecting larger animals which might threaten them. Hester smashed, squashed or swatted every single bug that came within reach. She even veered off to destroy any insect which drew her ire, and the elf began to seriously doubt the wisdom of bringing her along. How could any species kill so indiscriminately? What sort of hate did humans harbor that drove them to end the lives of creatures doing them no harm?

It wasn't that elves refrained from killing. They were as omnivorous as humans, and they would routinely wipe out infestations of pests in their homes. An elf would certainly swat a biting or stinging insect which threatened him or had the temerity to feast upon his flesh. But an elf wouldn't crush a harmless beetle simply for being in his path, let alone chase one down to squash it underfoot. The human desire to end lives for no reason was disconcerting.

Hester's bloodlust was so distracting that Inigo never heard the giant lizard maneuvering its bulk through the tall grass. He was walking one moment, watching as his hateful companion smote every small creature in her vicinity, and the next had him flat on his back, claws digging into his ringmail, a set of snapping jaws darting for his throat.

The lizard was nearly as big as the elf, and it was far more ferocious. Its serrated teeth held chunks of rancid meat from its previous meals, and its bite meant death by horrible, gangrenous infections. Had it not been for the exceptional skill of the elvish armorers, the scythe-like claws would've easily disemboweled Inigo.

The elf thrust his left forearm under the vile-smelling maw, forcing the snout upward. This not only improved the air quality for Inigo but gave him a chance to draw his dagger. He blindly stabbed at the beast, but his blade glanced off the thick scales on the lizard's flailing legs. The ringmail prevented the claws from piercing his flesh but did nothing to cushion the repeated impacts.

Inigo felt one of his lower ribs crack under the pummeling, a hot spike searing its way into his side. He struck with the dagger again and again, but the thick scales thwarted his counterattacks. Finally, one of the predator's swipes tore the blade from his grasp. The great lizard reared up, preparing to deliver a killing bite, and it seemed to be surrounded by an aura of fire.

The reptile bellowed in agony, flopping backward off the stricken elf. It rolled violently in the grass, attempting to extinguish the flames coursing over its scaly hide. The human bashed it with her walking staff, each hit striking more sparks, lighting more fires — in the midst of a prairie filled with dry, volatile grass. The woman was utterly mad!

"Stop!" the elf croaked as the greedy flames decided the dead grass would make a better meal than the flailing lizard. Hester never hesitated in her fiery assault on the reptile, not that it would've mattered. The winds sweeping over the plain whipped the small blazes into a furious inferno in a matter of moments.

Inigo forced himself to his feet, wincing at the molten dagger in his side. He dashed after the human, who was still pursuing the beleaguered predator. All around him, the fire began to roar, sending choking smoke into the air.

The elf grabbed the woman, scooping her up like a screaming, cursing, spitting child. Sprinting like the fires of Hell were licking at his posterior, he carried her toward the Forest of Despair. It was an eternity away, but it was their only chance at survival.

Chapter 12

Feather and Renato emerged from the forest less than a mile from the southern gates of Gunnar's Rest. Their armor glinted with crimson and orange highlights in the morning sun as Feather Coonslayer directed her faithful steed onto the gigantic road. The opossum disliked the bright direct light of the sun, but he obeyed without hesitation. The journey to the gate took forever to Feather's racing mind, for she knew her destiny awaited her within those titanic stone walls.

"How could the humans build something so magnificent, Renato?" she wondered, utterly in awe of the curtain wall. "Those must be the highest walls in the world. But why do some parts of the walls look like breasts?"

The jack, if he held any opinions on the height of the walls or the shape of the towers, declined to comment. Instead, he trundled onward, his keen nose sniffing in the smells of the giants who normally used this large path. This entire area reeked of danger, and his body thrummed like a taut bow from apprehension, his instincts demanding that he flee and hide or lie down and pretend he had died. The stink of a freshly dead, and therefore delicious, skunk called to him from the brush to his left, and his mouth filled with saliva as he envisioned tearing gobbets of putrefying flesh from the carcass. Everything the opossum knew told him to leave this giant, stinking road and tuck into that nice dead skunk before passing out in a bush. The only reason he had for remaining on this terrifying trail was riding on his broad back.

Feather, recognizing her steed's disquiet, muttered a few soothing platitudes. Her firm, gentle tone, rather than her words, calmed the jack. He continued onward, heeding her commands, but the sprite prepared to dismount and lead him once they neared the guards. She was just thankful there were no milling crowds awaiting entrance into the settlement. Renato was as well trained as she could make him, far braver than any wild opossum she'd ever encountered, but she knew she was an amateur compared to the true knights. Perhaps, in this city, she could find someone willing to teach her how to better handle a steed.

Captain Phil McCracken was leaning against his guard tower and sipping a cup of coffee, that foul-tasting, hot black bean broth that somehow seemed to wake even the groggiest soldier, when the strangest sight waddled into view. At first, he thought he had ergot poisoning again. Then, one of his guards' jaws dropped in shock.

"Cap'n, what the Hell is *that*?" the slack-jawed soldier asked.

'That' appeared to be a fairy, sprite or some other Wee Folk riding an opossum. Both rider and steed were clad in homemade armor. The damn 'possum wore loricated platemail fashioned from bits of turtle shells. Scalemail, made from what actually appeared to be scales, covered the fairy, though its shimmering, iridescent dragonfly wings protruded from its back. Atop the fairy's head was an acorn shell, polished to a gleaming luster. Its left arm carried a box turtle shell as a shield, and if McCracken wasn't much mistaken, a blasted crawdad claw had been formed into a gauntlet. The Wee One even had a tiny sword in a scabbard at its right hip, and a variety of small weapons strapped to the armored opossum's sides.

"Gonna be a strange day, boys," the captain of the guard remarked as the oddest cavalryman in the world reined its mount to a halt a respectful distance away.

Feather hadn't realized humans were quite this big. Her little heart was racing like a squirrel's as she slid out of her saddle. What was she doing here? Everything was sooo big, especially the terror gripping her stomach in its icy fist. She should leave, go back to the forest and forget all about this insane quest of hers—

Stop it! she commanded herself. *I am Feather Coonslayer, and I will not be afraid!*

Willing her voice not to crack, she announced, "Greetings, guardians. I am Feather Coonslayer, first of my clan, and I mean you no harm."

The titan towering over her, drinking from a cup she could nearly bathe in, smiled. Her heart quailed a bit at the size of his eyeteeth. He could easily snap her up in one bite. "Welcome to Gunnar's Rest, milady," he thundered cheerfully. "I am Phil McCracken, captain of the guards. What brings you to our fair town?"

Feather's heart slowed in relief. The humans, or at least the one who seemed to be the leader, appeared to be friendly here. "I am on a quest, Captain Phil McCracken," she intoned.

As if expecting her response, the captain nodded. "You'll be looking for Joel, then?"

She hadn't the slightest clue who this Joel might be, but she responded, "Indeed, Captain. Would you be so kind as to direct me to his dwelling? Also, I require forage for Renato."

"Uh, Renato? Oh, your 'possum!" McCracken blurted. "Right, uh, I'm fairly certain there's some garbage cans around the corner. All the other 'possums around here *love* garbage."

"You have my thanks, Captain Phil McCracken," Feather responded happily. "May your clan number as many as the leaves in the forest."

"Right back atcha, Feather," he replied warmly. "Say, if things don't work out with Joel, feel free to stop back by. We could use someone with your moxie around here."

The sprite didn't know what 'moxie' was, but the human's tone suggested it was intended as a compliment. "I shall keep your offer in mind. Now, if you would be so kind as to direct me to Joel's home, I will trouble you no further."

"I'll do you one better, milady," McCracken said. "I'll escort you there myself. After your mount eats his fill, of course. Boys, mind the store."

Together, the human and sprite walked around the corner, where several enormous metal containers sat. The stench wafting from them turned Feather's stomach, but Renato seemed overjoyed by the aromas of rot and decay. The captain gently laid one of the cans on its side and stepped back. Disgusted by the miasma emanating from the container, Feather turned her steed loose and stood beside the human. The jack dashed over to the refuse, feasting on spoiled meat and bits of rotten fruit.

"Quite the mount you've got there, milady," McCracken opined. "Can't say as I've ever seen a fairy riding a 'possum before."

"*Sprite*," she bristled, shuddering at being mistaken for one of those vile *things*.

"Sorry. I'll be honest: I've never been around any of the Wee Folk before," the human admitted. "No offense intended."

Feather flushed in horror. Had she really just spoken to the human so disrespectfully? "None taken, Captain. My apologies for my tone. Fairies are the mortal enemies of my people."

"I see my hoof-in-mouth disease is acting up again," McCracken muttered. "So, why do sprites and fairies hate each other?"

"Fairies are evil, bloodthirsty terrors," Feather answered, the mere thought of her clan's foes sending battle lust coursing through her veins. "They try to take our territory, inhabit our homes and steal our food. Everything we create, they attempt to destroy."

"Why?"

"No one knows," she replied sadly.

This was not entirely accurate. The feud between fairies and most of the other Wee Folk is reasonably well documented in Chapter 50: *Wee Wars*, of *The Adventurer's Almanac*. (This is, of course, not to be confused with Chapter 238: *The Wee Wars*, a compendium dedicated to the extended conflict between two rival chamberpot manufacturers which subsequently caused the Kegoboozia Civil War.)

Fairies, by nature, are carnivores. Their teeth and digestive tracts are similar to those found in several species of piranha, oddly enough. Unlike sprites, their main territorial rivals, fairies simply cannot digest plant matter. This inability to supplement their diet, coupled with their explosive reproduction rates, drives the entire fairy population to live a nomadic lifestyle, devouring every living animal in sight as they move — like locust swarms.

Rumors amongst the other Wee Folk insist that fairies are cannibalistic, even to the extent of hunting other Wee Folk. These tales are partially based on fact; however, it should be mentioned that the sprite the fairies devoured had been killed by a hawk and was already dead when the fairies ate the corpse. And the hawk. And the hawk's nestlings.

To differentiate between sprites, pixies and fairies — the three major species of winged Wee Folk — one need only look at the wings. Sprites possess sets of wings resembling those of dragonflies, dual pairs of shimmering, often transparent airfoils. This gives sprites the ability to hover, fly backwards and change directions at will. They can fly faster than any of their counterparts, but this speed comes at the expense of energy consumption. Sprites must consume vast quantities of food to provide the power for their wings.

The wings of pixies most closely emulate the lobed wings found on mayflies. The shape provides superior lift and flight stability and allows pixies to glide for short distances, but at the cost of maneuverability.

Fairies have scaly wings similar to those found on butterflies or moths. Like a butterfly, they seem to tumble haphazardly through the air. This makes fairies difficult targets for most predators, but it also means they fly more slowly. Unlike sprites and pixies, fairies can glide for long distances to conserve energy.

"Sounds about like everyone else," McCracken commented. "Everyone fights, but it seems like no one knows why. Sure as shit don't stop the fighting, though."

The sprite and the human fell into a melancholy silence for a few moments, until Renato finished his foray into the fascinating realm of rancid meat. The opossum waddled back to Feather's side, a slab of green ham clamped firmly in his teeth. The stench made his mistress gag as she flitted into her saddle, but he was perfectly content.

Ignoring the stink, McCracken led Feather and Renato through Gunnar's Rest. He happily gave the spriteknight a rundown of the various sights and spectacles the town had to offer as they passed by shops and confused pedestrians. The armored opossum drew wide-eyed stares everywhere they went.

They stopped beside a shiny metal statue of a massive human perched atop a stone pond. Feather marveled at the ability of these humans to bend something as strong as metal so expertly to their will. This, the captain explained, was a fountain built to commemorate Gunnar, founder of the city. It awed the sprite, but the sight of the bird droppings upon it saddened her deeply. Like so much else in their settlement, the humans seemed to take the magnificence of the fountain for granted. How could they live in a place of wonders, where stone and metal did their bidding, and not care?

"Why does no one clean the statue?" she asked of her host.

McCracken shrugged. "No one wants to do it for free, I reckon. Costs money to pay someone to do it, and the town council's so tight they'll squeeze a coin 'til it's the size of a dinner plate. That, and it'd have to be done fairly often; birds ain't exactly known for using chamberpots."

"Is something burning?" Feather asked in alarm. Her nose detected smoke, and smoke meant fire. Like all creatures of the forest, sprites are viscerally terrified of fire.

"Yeah. Some numbskull burned down the tavern last night. If I catch that idiot, I'll have him in irons for months. Pert near burnt half the city to the ground," the captain grumbled as they headed west.

Feather was confused. "Someone set a fire? On purpose?"

Again, the human shrugged. "Don't know that it was intentional, milady. If it's the fool I think it was, he probably didn't mean to cause as much trouble as he did."

"Humans are strange sometimes," she observed. "You live surrounded by wonders, yet you don't seem to appreciate them."

McCracken nodded. This little gal was pretty sharp for someone who rode around on a damn 'possum. Half of his job was preventing city idiots who didn't appreciate anything they had from hurting themselves or others. The other half was defending the city from attack by idiots who didn't appreciate anything they had.

Brightening, he inquired, "Little lady, are you hungry? Smokey's Inn has the best barbeque in town!"

She cocked her tiny head. "What is 'barbeque'?"

Chapter 13

Gorak was awake long before the sun rose. After carefully stoking the fire, he padded stealthily outside. His new friend's dooryard was large enough to perform the Warrior Ritual, he decided, so he set Skullcrusher aside and began to stretch his stiff muscles.

Facing the east, the troll eased into a crouch, as though straddling a horse. He extended his left arm in a slow punch at an invisible foe, following it with a strike from his right elbow. This turned into a gradual kick at the enemy to the north, coupled with an eye gouge. The southern attacker received a mule kick to his chest, and a throat punch as he fell to the ground. Lunging glacially to the west, Gorak drove a knee into a fourth foe's belly.

Beset by more imaginary attackers, the troll snatched up his war hammer. He lashed out to the northwest, the southeast, the southwest, and the northeast, all while whirling like a dervish. Skullcrusher and Gorak were two parts of the same whole, destroying any who dared to face him with savage blows and graceful pirouettes.

An hour and several scores of fictitious enemies later, the sweat-soaked troll brought the ritual to a close. He settled into a cross-legged sitting position, his mighty hammer balanced reverently across his thighs. Gorak's eyes drooped shut as he reflected upon his performance of the ritual and the challenges of the day ahead. Opening his mind, he asked his ancestors to guide him back to the Right Path.

He sat there waiting for their answer as the sun peeked over the curtain wall protecting the town. They remained conspicuously silent. The ancestors had never once spoken to Gorak; he was beginning to suspect they never would. Even before his fall from grace, they had ignored him.

Had they known all along that he would be an outcast?

Gorak opened his eyes, refusing to give that question any further consideration. He stood, slung his weapon across his back, and strode back into the house. His new friend still slumbered. The cancer, Gorak knew, was weakening the human badly. Soon enough, even sleep wouldn't help.

The troll retrieved some fish from the smoker. It was still warm, and the woody scent set his mouth to watering. He bit into the meat, finding it to be chewy and good. Better, even, than the dried ram flanks his mother had made. This human was full of surprises.

He was just finishing this bite of breakfast when he heard Jeremy stirring. The old man looked the worse for wear but seemed in a fine mood.

"Good morning, friend," the angler said. "Are you hungry? I'm in the mood for some barbeque and beer."

Gorak nodded happily. Beer and meat for breakfast? This human thought like a troll.

Jeremy slipped on a pair of boots and led the way to a place he called Smokey's Inn. "I know Smokey quite well," Jeremy informed Gorak as they sauntered along a cobblestone street. "He buys quite a bit of my catch, you see.

"You'll love the inn, friend. The dining hall is big enough for even someone your size, and the food! You've never had barbeque like this."

Which was certainly true. Tomatoes, a primary ingredient in barbeque sauce, do not fare well in the Highlands. Gorak had never tasted the ambrosia that is a slow-simmered, hardwood-infused, spicy sauce slathered onto prime cuts of steak and brisket.

Smokey's Inn, despite the early hour, was already bustling. Many of the patrons were obviously regulars, and they waved cheerfully at Jeremy as he and Gorak entered the enormous dining room. Unfamiliar yet alluring odors teased their way up the troll's sensitive olfactory organ. If this was what barbeque smelled like, Gorak thought, it was a crime against his people that they had never had any.

Jeremy led Gorak to a table in the corner. The troll sat gingerly upon the floor, sliding up to the smallish table. A human maiden in a short pink dress materialized at his elbow, removed a pencil from behind her ear, and eased herself into the chair beside Gorak. She laid a small scrap of parchment upon the table and gazed expectantly at the new patrons.

"Whatcha gonna have, boys?" she asked through her nostrils. She was chewing a wad of pink stuff with her mouth open, and the smacking sounds the goo made were like a grater drawn across the troll's eardrums.

"We'll start with brisket and beer, Flo," Jeremy answered. He seemed to be immune to her horrid voice and cud-chewing. She tipped the old man a wink and flounced away, jamming the writing utensil back behind her ear. Flo bellowed their order in the general direction of the bar, and Gorak had to suppress a wince.

"Her voice puts the war cries of many troll warriors to shame," he muttered to Jeremy. "But she doesn't smell human. What *is* she?"

Jeremy chuckled. "That's our Flo. She's been a waitress here in Gunnar's Rest for as long as I can remember. My grandfather used to tell me stories about her, but she hasn't aged a day."

Gorak found this even more disconcerting. Magic of any sort made him nervous. Immortal waitresses were far beyond his ken. Trolls, for the most part, have little talent for magic.

Watching Flo flit from table to table, Gorak realized that there were times he couldn't see her move. One moment she stood at a distant table, speaking with an old man missing an eye. The next, she was back at the bar, fetching drinks, yet she hadn't taken a single step. Could this strange woman teleport?

With such abilities, this Flo could be an unstoppable force. No warrior could hope to stand against an enemy capable of simply appearing anywhere on the battlefield. Her voice could easily penetrate the din of combat. And as she demonstrated by carrying a massive slab of meat to a crowded table, she was possessed of prodigious strength. Why was she simply serving customers?

Gorak mentioned these thoughts to his companion. The elder shrugged. "She's our Flo," he replied. "She does what she wants, friend. Her reasons are her own."

Unsatisfied with this response but unwilling to push the matter further, the troll fell into a pensive silence. Flo appeared with tall mugs of ale, vanished, and stepped back into reality bearing steaming plates of meat. The aroma which winked into existence with her was so heavenly Gorak was certain he'd died and gone to G'Varnsk, the fabled heavenly hall of his ancestors.

The first bite was sweeter than the ripest fruit, more glorious than Gorak's finest battle, and more comforting than the softest breast. The troll had never tasted such wonder. Juices ran down his chin, soaking his beard, but he couldn't have cared less. Unknown flavors exploded like dwarven bombs on his palate, lighting a fire within him that threatened to consume his very soul in an orgy of delicious, succulent meat and sauce.

All thoughts of the mysterious Flo were blasted from his mind. There was only the plated perfection and Gorak's need to consume it. He gorged himself upon this ambrosia, washing it down with heavy draughts of the frothy nectar in his mug. His plate never emptied and his ale never ran dry until he was too full to cram another bite of meat down his gullet.

It was then that he realized he had drawn a crowd. The human patrons were gathered round, exchanging coins and goods, wagering on his ability to consume food. As he gently pushed his plate aside, a chorus of cheers erupted from the victors. Even the losers seemed excited by the end of the troll's breakfast.

Flo settled into the chair beside him. "Beat the record," she remarked. "Nice job. Here's yer bill, boys."

Jeremy placed several coins on the table. "Keep the change, Flo." She disappeared. The money also vanished. Several of the patrons clapped Gorak on the back, congratulating the troll on shattering the former champion's record. Gorak looked to his mentor, confused by the praise.

The angler explained, "Smokey's Inn has a competition, friend. Whoever eats the most in one sitting gets their name on the board over there." He pointed at a wall behind the bar. "The previous winner didn't eat half as much as you."

Gorak was even more perplexed. "People here prize the ability to eat vast amounts of food? That is a competition amongst humans?"

"Humans will bet on *anything*. We're a highly competitive race."

The troll had to laugh. Humans were such odd creatures sometimes.

Chapter 14

The dining hall was extremely noisy, and it was giving Al a headache. The bruises on top of his cranium probably weren't helping either. The food smelled delicious, and the place sounded friendly as Nissan and Al found a table. Al wasn't sure what was going on across the room, but judging by the dozen or so guys standing and hooting, it was pretty exciting. There was even some gambling taking place, and Al felt that familiar itch drawing his hands to his empty pockets.

"Don't even think about it," Nissan snapped. "We don't have time for you to go lose money you don't have. We will eat, and then we will leave. Give me any further trouble, and you won't live long enough to regret it."

"Yeah, yeah," Al muttered. "I get the point."

The rogue placed his hand on the pommel of his sword. "Not yet, mage."

"See how brave you are when I set this place on fire," Al grumbled under his breath.

His mood spoilt, the wizard sulked. He toyed idly with a silver fork, fantasizing about using it to disembowel the rich asshole with the sword. While he was on fire. *Lots* of fire. A woman in a pink dress appeared at his elbow and

Al's heart stopped. In his mind's eye, he could see her true form and what Al saw almost made him shit his robes.

"Whatcha gonna have, mac?" the being disguised as a waitress asked in a nasal voice.

Al could only stare, too petrified to unlock his jaw. Her eyes narrowed suspiciously, and Al felt her summon power beyond his wildest dreams. Then, Nissan ordered steak, sausage and beer for both of them. The being departed, literally winking out of reality through a rift. The horrors he saw on the other side would give him nightmares for weeks.

"What is wrong with you, magician?" Nissan snarled. "You're staring into space like a doddering imbecile. Close your mouth, at least."

"You... you didn't see her?" Al asked.

"The waitress?" the rogue said. "Of course, I saw her, fool. Everyone sees her. By the Nine, of all the wizards in the world, I get stuck with a moron who's never seen a serving wench before."

"Right," Al murmured. "Just a waitress. Just a waitress." A cheer went up from the crowd across the room. More money was exchanged as wagers were settled. The crowd parted, and Al saw a familiar form. Broad back, big horns, orange Mohawk, bright green skin... It was the troll from the jail cell. A half-assed plan began to form in Al's mind.

Nissan huffed, "Look at that beast. I can't believe they allow things like that in here. Probably carries some horrible plagues."

"Nah. Trolls are pretty clean," Al countered.

"What would *you* know of cleanliness, wizard?" the rogue snorted. "You reek of your own filth. You wear shoes that have no soles. Your clothing hasn't encountered soap in weeks."

"Yeah, so I know what dirty looks like, jerk," Al spat. "You could be less of a prick, you know."

"Insult me once more, wizard," Nissan hissed. "My patience is at an end."

Al Ucard was never very good at keeping his big trap shut. It had gotten him into constant trouble. A smarter man might've learned to rein in his tongue. As previously mentioned, Al wasn't that man.

"Eat shit, you stuff-shirted bitch."

Before Nissan could react, Al flipped the table onto the silver-spoon-fed bastard and fled. Bellowing curses, the rogue erupted from his chair and drew his sword. Al dove over a nearby table, flattening several squawking patrons and spilling beer and food as Maxima thunked into the thick oak behind Al's feet. The mage leapt to his feet, cramming a chicken leg into his mouth, and rushed toward the troll, Nissan hot on his heels.

Al tore through the dining hall like a tornado, flinging chairs, mugs of ale, plates and discarded rib bones at his pursuer. He never looked back, but he could hear Nissan swearing and sputtering and tripping over the trail of debris. He heard the blade whistle through the air, felt it ruffle the small hairs on the back of his neck, and then he was diving over the startled troll.

"Help me! That asshole's trying to kill me!" Al bellowed around a mouthful of stolen chicken, keeping the big green monster between himself and the enraged, beer-soaked, barbeque-sauce smeared rogue.

"Friend of yours?" Jeremy asked cheerfully.

"No," Gorak replied. "Why does the other human wish to slay you, wizard?"

"He has impugned my honor for the last time!" Nissan snarled. "I will have his head for his impertinence!"

"Not here you won't," Flo stated, materializing at Nissan's side. "Put that weapon up, mac. Settle your hash later."

The well-dressed man glared at the waitress. "Do not think to order me about, wench! No mere woman—"

Al watched the being's eyes flare with rage. There was a flash of power that sent chills down his spine, and the being swatted Nissan in the chest with a contemptuous backhanded slap. It barely exerted less effort than was required to flick a booger a few feet, but the effects were far more dramatic.

Everyone else saw Flo draw back and throw a roundhouse punch. The rogue flew across the room, smashing a table to kindling. Nissan was knocked out by the landing, but not seriously harmed. Flo glared at Al as he cowered behind the massive troll. Like a flaming candle dropped into a powder keg, the inn erupted in a chaotic melee.

An enraged shout cast the entire inn into a silence impregnated with a sense of doom. In the doorway, looking resplendent in his polished armor, was Phil McCracken, captain of the guard. The captain's jaw clenched as his eyes locked on the mage.

"Oh, crap," Al mumbled.

Chapter 15

The Forest of Despair was a cool, if slightly smoky, sanctuary compared to the raging blaze tearing across the Jane Plain. It also wasn't very despair inspiring, in Hester's opinion. She and the elf had plunged deeply into its shady interior to escape the worst of the prairie fire's wrath.

They were singed, but alive. They were also short on supplies and arrows. The lizard had torn the straps of Inigo's quiver and pack, and neither he nor Hester had noticed until they'd entered the forest's green embrace. The arrows, his supplies and his dagger had all been lost to the inferno.

Once he'd realized he was partially disarmed, the elf had grown increasingly hostile toward his traveling companion. He blamed her for starting the fire with her staff. Of course, he hadn't complained much when she'd battled the stupid lizard off of his ungrateful hide.

He'd been driving them mercilessly through the woods, and his relentless pace was taxing Hester's untrained body. His dour silence was straining her patience. She hated the forest and would've gladly burned it all down around herself if she didn't hate the taste of smoke.

"I need a rest, elf," she spat as they topped a rise. "Stop."

Inigo furiously shook his head. "We need to keep moving, human. If the forest begins to burn, we shall be hard pressed to flee it."

Hester halted. "I said, we need to stop."

The elf rounded on her. "We cannot rest yet. What part of that did you fail to grasp?"

"Core concept, I suppose," she retorted. "I'm tired and my feet hurt. We need to rest."

"No," Inigo countered. "*You* need to rest. You are soft, human. You have allowed your body to become weak, like so many humans do. I have no time or patience for your enfeeblement. You will keep pace with me, and rest when I rest, or I will leave you behind."

Without another word, he spun on his heel and continued his frenetic plunge through the forest. Angry, but terrified of being left alone in these strange woods, Hester marshaled her reserves and followed.

They hadn't gotten far when Hester triggered the trap.

One second, she was tromping along behind the damn elf. An instant later, she was hanging upside down by her right ankle with her robes draped over her head and her undergarments on full display. Blinded by her own clothing, she squirmed and swore at the elf to cut her down.

Inigo was otherwise preoccupied. All around them, concealed trapdoors had burst open, spewing forth a horde of goblins. They were armed with rusty farm implements, bone clubs and knives, daggers made from bits of flint, and primitive wooden spears. The creatures were malnourished, judging by their protruding ribs and saggy skin, but Inigo was outnumbered by at least fifty-three fighters.

The Adventurer's Almanac, unfortunately, has very little information of the habits of the forest goblins — mostly because all of our researchers sent to seek them out mysteriously disappeared, never to be heard from again. Legend has it that the little creatures will eat anything, or anyone, unlucky enough to wind up in their territory, so the *Almanac* encourages extreme caution to those traveling through the Forest of Despair's southern reaches.

Inigo remained still and hissed at Hester to be silent. She, predictably, continued to harangue him. The elf held up his hands in surrender, and said, "Who speaks for your clan?"

A goblin smeared with stripes of red paint stepped forward, brandishing the thighbone of some large animal, possibly a horse or cow. "Whatchu want, meat?"

"I seek only peaceful passage through your lands, in accordance with the treaty between your species and mine," Inigo replied. He was bluffing. There was no such treaty between elves and any race of goblins, let alone these backwoods yokels.

"Treaty?" the goblin sneered. "Ain't no treaty, meat. We's hungry, and ain't got time for talkin'. Why don'tchu just put down your weapons, and make it easy?"

"I say there is an accord, goblin," Inigo snapped. "Harm me, and the war will begin once more. My people will show yours no mercy, should you slaughter a member of the ruling house."

"Oho! Got us an upper class bit of meat, we do!" the goblin guffawed. "Bet he's nice and tender!"

The bluff hadn't worked. Inigo whipped his swords from their sheaths, using the blades to slice through the rope supporting Hester. As she dropped in a griping heap, he dashed behind a tree. Spears burrowed into the ground where he had stood and gouged holes in the bark of the tree. Leaving Hester to fend for herself, the elf launched himself into combat.

Goblins swarmed him, lashing out at him with their makeshift weapons. Few of them scored any hits at all, but none could penetrate his skillfully crafted armor to do more than bruise him. He was in constant motion, striking here, feinting there, every attack slaying or disabling one of the little grayish-green fiends until the loamy soil on which he stood ran red with blood.

Hester had found herself in the middle of a herd of weird little demons. She was beaten and cut, beset on all sides, but most of all, she was angry. Screaming in fury, she started whacking the diminutive bastards with the Staff of Flameyness. Sparks flew and several of the goblins ran away, their hides ablaze with magical fire. Hester, of course, chased the poor things, continuing to pummel them.

All around her, the dry leaves and deadfall began to smolder and burn.

The goblin leader immediately grasped the predicament in which his clan had found itself. These bigger creatures were not only better fighters, they were about to burn his territory to cinders Did the female not care that she, too, would surely perish?

"Stop!" he cried at the woman with the stick. "You'll burn us all, you idiot!"

"Fine by me!" Hester shrieked, continuing to set his people on fire. "Threaten to eat me, you little shits? I'll burn your whole stupid forest down around me!"

"Run!" the goblin leader bellowed. He turned tail and sprinted away as fast as his stubby legs could carry him as the forest fire was born.

Inigo suddenly discovered that he was no longer under attack. The goblins — the living ones, at least — were routed. A spark of pride warmed the elf. He was really warm, come to think of it. A little too warm, truth be told. "Not again," he whispered. He turned slowly at the infernal roar from behind him.

To an elf, a member of a race which teaches its young to forge a connection with trees at an early age, what Inigo beheld was a horror beyond imagining. The insane woman had created his worst nightmare, and he was momentarily paralyzed by terror at the sight of the conflagration. It was only when Hester shoved him out of her way that the trance was broken. Tears in his eyes which had nothing to do with the smoke, the elf fled.

Chapter 16

Feather had never seen such destruction. Or so much food left to waste. The brawl between the giants had left their furniture broken and scattered. Drink soaked into the floorboards. Lovely smelling meat lay everywhere. She was horrified by it all. Renato was thrilled, and quickly left her side to gorge himself on the floor-meat.

Phil McCracken, captain of the guard, stormed over to Al. "Arson wasn't enough, son?" he snapped. "Decided to wreck up the best barbeque joint in town, too?"

Al stared at his feet. His nose was bleeding from a sucker punch, but he didn't have the energy to staunch it. The captain somehow had the ability to make him feel like an unruly five-year-old. "Sorry, Cap."

"Sorry doesn't cut it!" McCracken growled, a vein pulsing at his temple. "Look at this place! Do you have any idea how much damage you caused at the Boarskull? You almost burned down an entire block of my town!"

"It was an accident," Al muttered forlornly. "You gotta believe me, Cap. I didn't mean for that to happen."

McCracken snorted like a bull and pivoted to lay his basilisk gaze upon Gorak. "I seem to recall you promising me you weren't going to cause trouble in my town."

The troll held the soldier's gaze. "I did not cause this fight, Captain. I defended myself, but I am not responsible for the battle."

"He speaks the truth," Jeremy said. "We were enjoying our breakfast when this young man," he gestured toward the mage, "interrupted our meal. He was fleeing the man with the feathered hat on the floor over there."

"You're saying that fop started this?" McCracken demanded. "That true, Flo?"

The waitress nodded. "Yep. He was trying to kill the wizard. Not entirely sure why. Fight broke out when the punk with the sword decided to mouth off to me."

The captain pinched the bridge of his nose. "Flo, are you telling me you started this mess?"

"He needed his butt kicked," she replied defiantly. "I ain't taking no lip from that jive turkey, Captain."

"Nothing's ever simple," McCracken lamented. "Fine. Whatever. What'd you do to piss off that guy, mage?"

Al shrugged. "The usual. Opened my big mouth. Also, it was his fault the tavern burned."

"I'll kill you!" Nissan shouted, driving his sword at Al's stomach. He'd moved so quickly no one had been able to stop him. The mage dove to the side and the blade slashed a new hole in his cloak. Al tumbled across the floor, drawing a frightened hiss from Renato.

Jeremy, however, hadn't been agile enough to evade the sword. The blade had entered his abdomen, carving through his liver and bursting from his back. The old man's jaw dropped in shock, and he grabbed at the sword, cutting his hands on the keen edge. Nissan gaped in horror as the innocent man he'd just impaled sank to his knees.

Nissan withdrew the blade with a slurp of blood and dashed away. Captain McCracken bellowed for the aid of any guards within earshot. Gorak hurled his war hammer with a furious roar, but his aim was poor. The massive stone head of the hammer smashed an enormous hole in the wall a few inches behind the fleeing rogue. Flo pressed a relatively clean rag to the bleeding wound as the misery he'd created seared itself into Al's brain.

"Save him," the mage begged of Flo. "Please."

The being shook its head sadly. "That is beyond my power, wizard. He will suffer less this way. Exsanguination is preferable to the cancer devouring him from within." To everyone else's ears, Flo simply said, "He ain't gonna make it."

Gorak knelt beside his dying friend. "I will not let this injustice go unpunished, *rasgul*. Your kindness will not be forgotten, and you shall be avenged."

Jeremy smiled through his pain. "Don't forget... to fish."

The light faded from his eyes. Though they hadn't known each other long, the troll wept for his friend.

McCracken laid a hand gently on the troll's shoulder. "We'll find him, son. You've got my word on that."

Gorak nodded curtly and got to his feet. His rage burning like a red sun within his gut, he grasped the front of the wizard's clothing and lifted the pathetic human off the ground. Gorak held Al's face within mere inches of his own and snarled, "You've killed a good and decent man. Where will your bastard companion go?"

"I don't know!" Al blurted, his feet dangling two feet off the ground. "Look, I'm sorry! I didn't mean for anyone to get hurt!"

"*Where?*" the troll roared, shaking the mage like a ragdoll. Spittle flew from his tusks as he bellowed, "*Where?*"

"Holy shit, I don't know!" Al cried, fear cracking his voice. "Stop, please!"

The troll was preparing to tear the mage apart when Captain Phil McCracken intervened. "Don't. Don't kill him. There's been enough blood spilt here already."

Gorak dropped the mage in a terrified heap. The landing apparently shook something loose in Al's head. "Joel," Al muttered. "That asshole was looking for Joel. Wanted me to take him to Joel."

"You will take me to this Joel," Gorak stated coldly. "We will find the human with the floppy hat, and when we do, I will destroy him for what he's done."

"No," McCracken said. "You'll allow my men and I to find the murderer. I won't have a troll going berserk on my streets. I won't have vigilantes waging war in my town. We'll find him, and we'll bring him to justice."

"You can't prevent him from avenging his friend," Feather piped up. She flew up to the top of a nearby table. "Where's the justice in that?"

The captain sighed. "Milady, as much as I can appreciate the desire to seek retribution, my duty is to the laws of this town. We don't condone vigilante justice here. You're not in the forest, or the mountains. Not any more. You're in my town, and you will abide by the town's rules. Understand?"

"I hear you," Gorak huffed. He stomped over to the wall, and wrenched Skullcrusher free. "I will not pursue this murderer within your walls. Should you fail to capture him, however, and he steps outside your town, I will not be bound by your idea of justice."

"Fair enough," McCracken relented. He didn't like it, but he wasn't about to argue with a righteously pissed off troll. Two of his guards arrived, panting slightly from their run, and McCracken rapidly filled them in on the situation and sent them to alert the guards on the walls. The captain was determined to bring in the killer before he stepped a single foot outside Gunnar's Rest.

"Anyone want anything?" Flo asked.

"Not now, Flo," McCracken sighed.

Gorak stood beside the cooling corpse of his rasgul for an eon, awaiting the arrival of the undertakers. Al spent the time alternately describing Nissan and his habits to the guards and silently mired in his own self-loathing and guilt. Flo cleaned up the mess the patrons had caused. Feather studied the strange green giant, carefully observing his grief. Renato, oblivious to everything else, happily feasted upon more of the yummy floor-brisket.

The moment McCracken stepped outside to speak to his men, Gorak picked up the mage by the scruff of his neck. "You will take me to Joel now."

"You promised the captain you wouldn't pursue Nissan," Feather said quietly.

"I vowed not to pursue the man who slew my *rasgul*," Gorak replied. "I said nothing of finding this wizard. And if this Nissan happens to arrive to see Joel while I am there and happens to attack me, his death shall be in defense of myself, and my vow to Captain McCracken shall remain unbroken."

"Classy," Al chuckled. "Can you put me down now?"

The troll dropped the mage. "Lead the way, wizard."

Rubbing his sore tailbone, Al blanched. "Now? You want to go right now? Shouldn't you see to your friend's body or something?" Gorak growled softly and Al sputtered, "Uh, right! Let's go!"

The troll and the human mage ducked out the back door. Feather Coonslayer, intrigued by the enormous green monster, mounted her faithful steed and followed.

Chapter 16

All around them, the world burned. Everywhere they looked, the inferno raged. They ran, choked by smoke, blinded by tears. Hester lost count of the number of times she fell, picked herself up, and kept fleeing the Hell she had created. Somehow, she'd managed to keep up with the elf in their panicked flight.

Although she'd never admit it, she was beginning to regret setting the forest ablaze, mostly because trying not to die in a fire sucked. A lot. The smoke reeked and she couldn't smell anything else. The heat pulled the moisture from her throat and left her skin feeling as though it would split open at any moment. Every breath was agony.

For Inigo, the horror of the forest fire was the single worst event of his long life. He could hear the trees screaming in agony, but all else was the thunderous roar of the inferno. The elf had never known that fire *could* roar. Embers rained upon him, singeing his hair, scorching his clothes. His armor had gotten so hot that it was scalding his skin.

Worst of all, he knew he couldn't outrun the flames. His breathing was labored, and the reach of the blaze was wrapping around their path. The wind was pushing the flames faster than his feet could carry him. Soon, he and the human would die.

It was with this morbid thought in his head that Inigo Stormrunner watched the woman vanish. She simply disappeared, right before his watering eyes. He heard her shout in surprise, and he skidded to a halt. There, at his feet, was a dark hole edged with bits of sticks. The witch had fallen down one of the goblins' shafts. Desperate, Inigo jumped down the hole after her.

The tunnel was cramped and reeked of goblin piss. As badly as the ammonia stink burned in his nostrils, Inigo was grateful to be inhaling something besides smoke. The woman lay nearby, clutching her ankle and cursing the goblins' ancestors.

"They've likely saved our lives," the elf croaked, his voice hoarse from smoke inhalation. "We should keep moving." He felt a cool breeze on his face, coming from the tunnel fork to the left. "Fresh air comes from this way."

"My ankle hurts," she groaned.

"The tunnels are too low to walk," the elf pointed out. "You will not injure your ankle further by crawling. We must move, unless you'd rather suffocate."

Continuing to curse and complain, the woman began to crawl. Inigo followed her. Perhaps it was the smoke, but he found himself admiring the curve of her posterior. Yes, it was definitely the smoke. Elves did *not* have dalliances with lesser races.

They crawled for miles. Inigo saw no goblins, but he could occasionally hear the little fiends squeaking and chattering. They appeared to be in full flight, which suited the elf just fine. These cramped conditions favored the smallish goblins in combat.

Finally, Inigo and Hester emerged in a cavern. The elf could see light, glorious, wonderful light. He could also see water, cool and clear, pouring into a small pond within the cavern. Unfortunately, the soul-nourishing light also enabled him to see all of the damn goblins skulking about within the cave.

And if their furious hissing was an indication, they could see him as well.

"This will be unpleasant," Inigo sighed. "Prepare yourself, human," he suggested, helping her to her feet.

"They did this!" the thighbone-toting goblin shrieked, pointing at Hester and Inigo. "They started the burning!"

"Of course, we did," Inigo called as the horde advanced. "And we shall gladly burn everything within these warrens if you do not let us pass!"

The goblins hesitated. They were afraid, and the elf intended to use that fear. Inigo led Hester forward, smiling tightly as the little fiends took a step back. The human and the elf skirted the pool of clear water. The goblins were held at bay by fear, but Inigo knew they would eventually overcome that reticence. He and Hester had to get to the cave's mouth before their enemies decided the threat didn't exist.

They were within a few steps of the exit when disaster struck. The cave floor, polished by countless goblin feet and eons of running water, was slippery. Hester's injured ankle had given her a slight limp, and when her foot skidded on the slick rock, she was unable to catch herself. Before Inigo could even reach out to her, Hester landed on her rump and slid down the slope into the pool. There was a gigantic splash which sprayed droplets of water onto the stunned goblins.

There was a moment of doom-laden silence and then came the tittering of dozens of goblins. Thighbone hefted his club and cried, "Fire witch is wet! Kill them!"

Inigo suppressed a groan. The leader of the goblins was smarter than he looked. The elf's swords leapt into his hands as he sought higher ground amongst several large stalagmites, again leaving Hester to fend for herself.

Little green monsters swarmed Inigo's makeshift redoubt. Spears were driven between the stone teeth, rocks and skulls were lobbed over them, and all around him were hissing demonic faces. The elf hacked off the tips of the weapons, dodged the projectiles, and drove his armored boots into goblin jaws. His every move was automatic, born of decades of training and muscle memory.

The elf was dancing over broken spears and skulls, piling up goblin bodies like cordwood, but his strength was flagging. Skilled and disciplined though he was, Inigo knew there were simply too many of the vile beasts. He would just have to see how many of them he could send to the Underworld before he fell.

A lucky spear strike caught him in his wounded rib, and he staggered. Enervated by the agony, his left hand opened against his will and three feet of fine elven steel clattered to the stone floor. A flying rock clipped his left temple, and the elf saw two swords in his two right hands decapitating a pair of goblins. Bone clubs rained on him from all directions, and Inigo fell to his knees. Another blow to his head left him seeing a strange, flickering orange glow. There was a sound like screaming in his ears and his vision went dark.

A moment later, his brain restarted. There was still a flickering orange light, and he still heard screaming, but he was reasonably certain he was alive. The goblins were no longer attacking him, so the possibility existed that he was dead. The pain stabbing him as he regained his feet argued in favor of his still being alive, but the horrible cries of the damned and acrid stink of burning flesh suggested he was in some Hell or another.

Climbing over the pile of goblin carcasses closest to the light, the scene he witnessed cast more doubt on his status.

There in the water stood a goddess of death and fire. Her soaked clothing clung to nubile curves like a second skin. Drenched hair hung alluringly about a face made exquisitely beautiful by rage. Full lips were drawn back in a snarl, exposing teeth which glittered like diamonds in the firelight. She stormed through the shallow water, her staff breathing flames like a tiny wooden dragon, goblins scattering and burning in her wake.

The elf was stunned by her deadly beauty. Could this avatar of savage doom really be the same woman he'd been traveling with all day? How had he not seen this glorious side of her?

Inigo slapped himself. She was a *human*. A lowly, stinking human. Elves did *not* have romantic feelings for humans. So why couldn't he stop staring at her?

Below him, Hester stopped flailing about with the Staff of Flameyness. There were no goblins within her reach. "Yeah, you'd better run!" she yelled after them. "Cowards!"

Furious at being soaked in the cold water, her ass sore from her fall, and her ankle aching like it was filled with nettles, she made her way to the shore. The elf had holed up amongst a bunch of stalagmites and had killed his fair share of the tiny green bastards, which was all well and good, but he was staring at her in a way that made her feel tingly.

"You coming or what, elf?" she called, using the staff as a cane. "I've had enough of this stupid cave already."

Retrieving his weapon, Inigo made his way to her side. "Yes, we elves have never been enamored with caves. Or goblins."

"Yeah? What are you enamored with, elf?" Hester inquired coyly. Inigo's tongue refused to function properly, and she chuckled, "Cat got your tongue?"

"No," he managed to mutter.

"Good," she responded, wrapping her arms around him. She pressed her lips to his, and lightning coursed through his body. Quests could wait. She wanted him here and now, surrounded by burning corpses, on this wet cave floor. The elf stopped caring what was around them the moment he tasted her lips.

Chapter 17

"Are you certain this is the place we seek, human?" Gorak snapped. "It does not appear to be the home of a wealthy and powerful wizard."

Al rolled his eyes and sighed. "I'm telling you, this is the place. It's enchanted to look like it's abandoned."

"No, it's not," Feather disagreed from her saddle on Renato's back. "The enchantment is just there to encourage people to ignore it."

The mage stared at the sprite. "Didn't know sprites could see magic."

She shrugged. "You giants don't pay attention to much that's smaller than you are. Whoever cast that enchantment is really good. It's subtle enough to not be detected, but effective enough to turn most people away. Even Renato doesn't want to look at it."

"See?" Al said with a smirk. "Really good wizardry, Gorak. As in Joel."

"We shall see," the troll snorted, striding toward the seemingly abandoned domicile. His instincts were telling him that no one was here, that he was wasting his time, but both the wizard and the tiny one had insisted that his instincts were wrong. He continued on, and the clamoring of his instincts increased and waxed until he was close enough to realize that the holes in the roof and the neglected paint were faked. Gorak was in awe of the artistry involved in the charade, and he hesitated at the doorway.

If his instincts were so wrong about this place, could they be trusted to detect any booby-traps protecting the entrance?

The answer, of course, was no. Gorak knocked anyway, his heavy knuckles rapping rather gently upon the wood.

Al involuntarily cringed, expecting the troll to be vaporized by Joel's wards. Instead, the door opened to admit Gorak. The mage and the sprite rushed forward, and all of them stepped into a dimly lit foyer.

No sooner had they entered than the door slammed itself shut behind them. Al was effectively blind as his eyes strained to adjust to the dark. Gorak saw everything in varying shades of purples, reds and blues, depending on how much heat emanated from their surface. Feather's pupils dilated so quickly it was as though the light had never changed.

"Wow. Joel needs a maid," Al observed as his eyes finally caught up with the dark. "And bigger shelves for all of his books. Think that's the reason he called for help?"

"No," a raspy voice answered. "The tasks I require assistance to complete are of far more importance than mere cleaning. Have you retrieved my things from the cave of R'an D'om yet?"

"Uh, no," Al responded. "You didn't actually ask us to do that yet."

The wizened mage cocked his head slightly to the left. "I haven't? I could've sworn I had. Go to the cave, lay waste to the parasites inhabiting it, and bring back anything that looks important."

"Sure thing," Al replied. At Gorak's snarl, Al added, "You haven't seen a snappily dressed, pompous asshole with a floppy hat by any chance, have you?"

"I do not believe I have," Joel muttered. "Still, I have been busy, so it's hard to say for certain."

"He murdered Gorak's friend," Feather announced. "Please try to remember."

The old wizard stared incredulously at her. Then, he glanced at Al. "Do you see a sprite riding an armored opossum?"

"Yes," the troll replied. "Her name is Feather."

Joel breathed a sigh of relief. "Thank the Fates. For a moment there, I feared I had accidentally eaten peyote again."

"The man in the floppy, feathered hat," Gorak snapped. "Has he been here yet? We know he is looking for you. He killed my *rasgul* in cold blood, wizard."

"I do not recall speaking to this man," the wizard replied testily. "And I do not appreciate your tone."

"We will wait here for him, then," the troll announced. "He will arrive soon enough, and I shall deal with him."

"You will *not*!" Joel thundered, his eyes flashing with power. "This is my sanctuary, troll, and no one shall defile it with a blood feud!"

Before the warrior could speak, Feather cried, "You promised the captain you wouldn't pursue Nissan! It was one thing to seek Joel and take the chance of encountering the one who killed your friend, but to lie in wait for him would violate your vow."

Furious, Gorak opened his mouth to shout down the insect. Then, he closed his jaw with a clop. "You are right to rebuke me," he stated quietly. "In my lust for revenge, I have soiled what remains of my honor. We should leave."

"Are you going to get my stuff or not?" Joel demanded. "If not, then stop wastin my time and get the Hell out of my house! Who are you fools anyway?"

"We'll take the job," Al responded. "I'm Al Ucard, traveling wizard. The big green troll is Gorak Stonecrusher. The sprite is Featherwillow Coonslayer. The 'possum is Renato.

"So, what kinda crap do you have in the cave, anyway?"

Joel glared at the lesser mage as though he'd just blown his nose on the drapes. "That is none of your concern. A mage of your, ah, *quality* would have no use for any artifacts of mine."

Al recoiled from the insult. "You stuck up son of a whore! I'll show you quality, you—"

He was interrupted by an extraordinarily large and rough green hand clamping over his mouth. "Do not antagonize him," Gorak said softly. "You will only cost us our chance at glory."

"Yes, listen to the troll," Joel advised smugly. "You cannot hope to stand against me. I have had centuries to perfect my command of magic. You, however, dropped out of the academy and wander about performing parlor tricks and selling snake oil to fools even more pathetic than yourself."

Al's face burned with rage and shame. Joel was absolutely right, even if he was being a complete prick about it. "Go screw yourself," he muttered.

Joel chuckled. "About the level of discourse I would expect from a charlatan such as yourself. You are nothing, Al Ucard, and you never shall be more. You will always run away when you should stand and deliver, because you are a weak, undisciplined coward."

"That seems unnecessarily cruel," Feather opined with a moue of disappointment.

The wizard glowered down at her. "You are an even bigger fool. A sprite who wishes to be a knight. You think your pathetic armor will make you mighty. You chose one of the least combat worthy creatures in your entire forest for a steed. You are less than nothing, sprite. You should go back to your worthless little stump and raise another generation of your species to serve as food for more worthy creatures — such as toads!"

The sprite blinked back tears. Sensing his mistress's dismay, Renato let out a warning hiss. Joel was about to continue to tear into the poor Wee Folk when a knobby set of knuckles slammed into his nose with the force of an enraged mule's kick.

Squealing in pain and spurting blood from his snoot, Joel tumbled backward. The pain prevented him from focusing enough to cast a spell before Gorak seized Joel's throat and hauled the bloody wizard to his feet. The troll gripped Joel's bleeding nose between the horned knuckles of his first two fingers and twisted slightly. Joel gurgled in agony.

"You will not speak to the female that way again," Gorak growled. "Apologize, or I will tear your snout off. Do you understand?"

"Merfectly!" Joel cried. "Broke by dose!"

"I can easily break more things," Gorak mused, squeezing a bit tighter until the mage squeaked. "Make your choice."

"I'm sorry," Joel whispered.

The troll was unimpressed. "I can't hear you," he snarled, twisting his hand.

"*I'm sorry*!" Joel screamed. "Stop, damn you!" Gorak twisted harder. "Stop... please!"

"Better," Gorak replied, lightening his grip slightly. "I am going to release you now, wizard. Do not make me regret doing so. I can easily kill you before you cast one of your spells."

The troll turned the wizard loose. Joel flung himself away from Gorak with an outraged squawk. Al felt power blossom into a spell, saw Joel's lips begin to move, and heard the crackle of magic far beyond his own. Joel extended his finger toward the troll, preparing to cast something dire. Gorak was wrong about being fast enough to slay Joel before he could form a spell. The big troll didn't have a chance.

Without thinking, Al thrust his right hand forward, his forefinger, middle finger and pinky extended. He drew upon his limited access to power and yelled, "Shocker!"

A blue lightning bolt the thickness of horsehair leapt from Al's fingertips. The pathetic spell didn't even produce enough light to challenge the candlelight. It was as nothing compared to the sheer force Joel was capable of commanding. It was, however, aimed directly at Joel's crotch.

The wizard let out a high-pitched scream of agony as the tiny lightning caressed his groin. His spell dissipated as his will collapsed. Joel fell to his knees, grasping his aching testicles with both hands and mewling like a dying kitten.

"Uh, run!" Al yelled, dashing for the door. Once Joel recovered, there would be utter Hell to pay.

Wasting no words, Gorak and Feather followed Al. The troll had no idea how truly close to death he'd been, but he knew he'd narrowly dodged something very bad. Feather, on the other hand, had seen the spell Joel had woven. Had it been cast successfully, Gorak would've been reduced to a simmering pile of primordial ooze sloughing from a pile of bones. Al had saved Gorak's life.

Once the wizard had recovered, Feather feared his retaliation would be horrible and swift. Al may have saved the troll's life today, but he had likely doomed them all. Worse, there was no way Feather would be able to complete her quest.

Chapter 18

When Hester and Inigo left the goblin cave, they had emerged from the side of an enormous hill. Although not quite a mountain, it had acted as an effective firebreak. Everything they saw was lush and green. Birds flitted cheerfully through the air. Even the scent of smoke was almost nonexistent.

"This forest has a stupid name," Hester opined. "A few goblins don't exactly inspire desperation."

Inigo shook his head. "The Forest of Despair wasn't named after them. We should move, or we won't be out of the forest before dark."

She frowned. "What difference does that make?"

"You do not wish to meet the nocturnal creatures that inhabit these woods. Nor do you wish to encounter the reason for this forest's name."

"Whatever."

The hike was long, especially with Hester's injured ankle, which was now roughly the size of a grapefruit. It was slowing them down like an anchor lashed to her leg, forcing them to stop frequently so she could rest. At the reduced rate of travel, Inigo feared they would be unable to escape the trees before nightfall.

Even in Ka'El, the High Elves knew not to be caught within the Forest of Despair after dark. The legends described terrible beings which stalked these cursed woods at night, devouring everyone outside substantial shelter. These horrors could exsanguinate an elf in minutes and destroy an entire army before sunrise. No one knew exactly what they were, nor what they looked like, but the very notion of being trapped in the Forest of Despair after dark made Inigo's blood run cold.

Hester was angry. Her clothes were wet and chafing her in some remarkably unpleasant ways. Her ankle hurt like it was about to fall off. She was tired, but the elf wouldn't let her rest long enough. And to top it all off, she could've sworn she heard some of those stupid goblins shadowing them in the woods.

"Are we there yet?" she whined.

"No."

"Why don't we stop for a while, and mate some more?"

"Tempting, but no," Inigo sighed. "We must be outside the forest by nightfall. Once we're out of danger, it will be my pleasure to lay you down."

Gripping Inigo's hand, Hester drew him into a kiss. His brain ceased to function, consumed by a passion that scorched away all else in a cleansing fire. He forgot all about the need to flee the forest before dusk, and the reason that it was so important.

They lay intertwined on the forest floor, rolling and thrusting upon a bed of leaves. Hester had never felt so alive, so free and so utterly wonderful. Not even burning down a prairie and slaying scores of goblins had given her such a rush. Everything about the elf thrilled her in a way nothing else in her life ever had, and she was determined to ensure it never ended. She wasn't quite certain how she would accomplish that goal, however.

Inigo had no such thoughts. In fact, he was so overwhelmed by the sensations exploding from his groin that he wasn't thinking at all. Thinking could wait until sometime next century. Right now, the only thing that mattered was the exquisite softness of her body wrapped around his own.

Afterwards, she lay curled up in his arms, enjoying his warmth. Inigo drove his nose into her hair, inhaling her wondrous scent. He felt a fluttering at his crotch, but it was brief. His manhood, for now, was spent and she was nearly asleep. Her hair glittered like rubies in the light from the setting sun.

"No," he whispered. "Wake up and get dressed. We need to be ready."

"Fuhwha?" she mumbled. "Sleepy."

Inigo eased his arm from beneath her. Quickly, he donned his clothes and his armor. He was strapping on his swords when a skittering sound turned his bowels to ice water. The elf whirled to face it, weapons leaping into his hands, but he saw nothing. The dying light painted the world in gray. The skittering came again, once more behind him. Closer this time. He spun right, blade at neck height, but again found nothing.

Had he imagined it? Was he allowing legends and old wives' tales to cause his senses to run wild?

A strange goo dripped onto his outstretched sword. "Damn," he murmured, cursing himself for a fool. He'd forgotten to check the trees above him.

Hissing what almost sounded like words, the horrors dove at the elf from their arboreal perches.

Chapter 19

Feather, Gorak and Al had ceased their flight outside an abandoned apothecary shop. Thus far, Joel hadn't pursued them. The wizard was, of course, completely capable of waiting until they had been lulled into a false sense of security. He hadn't lived to be centuries old without developing patience. Sooner or later, there would be a reckoning, and Gorak regretted not smashing the wizard to a fine paste with his war hammer.

It would've been somewhat dishonorable to have slain a disabled opponent, but Gorak had done far worse. What was one more bloodstain on his honor? "We should go back," the troll stated. "We should finish this fight."

"Are you nuts?" Al snapped. "Do you have any idea how close you came to being turned to grease? You don't screw with mages that powerful, you idiot!"

Gorak shrugged. "No one has the right to disparage a female, particularly not a warrior. He needed a lesson in manners, and I was happy to administer it."

Feather blushed. "Thanks, Gorak. You honor me, but the wizard was right. I'm not a warrior. I killed a raccoon."

The troll snarled, "I will not stand here and listen to you give in to his insults! You defended your clan, did you not?"

"Yes, but—"

"Against a foe far larger and more powerful than yourself?"

"Yes, but—"

Gorak interrupted once more. "You defended your clan from an attacker, fought and slew an opponent who could've easily killed you, and here you stand, far from your home, searching for more honor and glory. You may be small, Feather Coonslayer, but a warrior's heart knows no size. Joel is a fool, and I will hear no more of his lies spill from your lips."

Feather nodded, the fire of her pride rekindled by the kind words of this gigantic monster. If a fighter of Gorak's status accorded her as an equal, then a warrior she was. She smiled, gazing up at her benefactor and defender — and was startled to see the face of a dead human staring out at her from the window of the abandoned shop. Involuntarily, she screamed.

Al pivoted to follow the sprite's gaze. "What in the Nine Blue Hells is that?"

Gorak turned and stared at the window's filthy, wavering glass. "It appears to be a window, human."

"You don't see it, do you?" Feather asked. Behind the glass, the corpse gnashed its teeth and pressed a rotting hand to the frame.

"Trolls aren't all that perceptive when it comes to magic," Al muttered, examining the phantasm. "It's a spirit of some sort. Not sure what kind, exactly, but I'm guessing it's a guardian ghost. I'm going in."

"Is that wise?" Gorak inquired doubtfully. "I cannot fight what I cannot see."

Al chuckled darkly. "You wouldn't be able to fight it if you could see it. It's incorporeal, so your weapons are useless against it. The ghost may be able to hurt you, but you won't be able to do shit to it."

"Neither will I," Feather stated. "Sprites can see magic, but I've never been able to use it very well. If you go in there, you'll be on your own, Al. Wait. Can't you enchant our weapons so we can hit the ghosts?"

Al rolled his eyes. "Sure, if I had a bunch of silver and a few weeks. Enchanting a weapon ain't like putting on a pair of socks, Feather. It's brutal, painstaking work, and the slightest mistake can cause the weapon to, well, *explode* a little."

The troll grimaced. "How does something explode a little?"

"It doesn't. It goes off like one of those bombs the dwarves are always using to dig their mines. It blows right the Hell up, and generally kills everyone in the area — which is why most mages don't try to enchant anything, ever. We like not dying in a fiery conflagration if we sneeze."

"Why don't we leave the spirit alone, then?" Feather asked. "It's not exactly hurting anything, is it?"

"People don't summon guardian spirits without a good reason," Al reasoned. "No, there's something in there worth protecting, ergo worth acquiring for ourselves. I'm going in!"

Before the sprite or troll could protest, Al burst through the door of the abandoned apothecary shop. The guardian spirit reacted, predictably enough, by tearing off its own face and shrieking like a banshee. Unimpressed, Al walked right through it, which was like strolling in cold rain for a moment. He extended his senses to fill the room, searching for whatever valuable things might've been stored there. The ghost continued attempting to be scary, but the jaded wizard simply kept ignoring it.

The dark interior of the shop was filled with multitudes of glass jars and vials filled with random things. Most of it was far past its prime, almost all of it was pretty well useless, and it was all covered in inches of dust. Al wandered about the room as though he were just a shopper, watching the ghost from the corner of his eye. As he headed toward the right, the spirit seemed to calm down. When he meandered to the left, it grew increasingly agitated.

Al smiled. Whatever this spirit was guarding was somewhere in the vicinity of the counter. He strolled past the raging ghost, hopped over the counter like a boy hurdling a bale of straw, and began searching under the counter.

As the ghost raved and gibbered, Al opened a plain wooden chest. There was a ring, a few baubles, but nothing which warranted its own guardian. They'd sell, however, so he slipped all of the loot into his pocket. The next chest held a few extremely valuable herbs — all of which were ruined from sitting in a box for so long.

The final chest bore a padlock the size of his head. "There's my bitch," Al chuckled happily. Directing his will at the box, Al attempted to discern its contents. He could sense an item of power, but he had no clue what it was, or what it did. "Screw it," he muttered, driving his will into the lock.

The tumblers were heavy, and rust had made them recalcitrant. Sweat broke out on Al's forehead as he called upon his magic to push against the corrosion. Straining, he felt them begin to shift before sticking harder than before. He took a steadying breath and redoubled his effort. His head began to throb terribly, and blood dripped from his nostrils.

Suddenly, the tumblers sprung into position. The lock snapped open with such force that it flopped off the chest like a fish and clattered to the floor. Wailing from the guardian spook reached an earsplitting crescendo as Al cracked the box open.

Inside the box, nestled within a bed of blood-red velvet, was a crystal. It was roughly eight inches long, as big around as a wine bottle, and cut into facets with unnatural precision. The gem's interior was cloudy, as though it were filled with mist, but it glowed with a hellish, pulsing purple light. Intrigued, Al grabbed the crystal.

A wave of coruscating energy erupted from the gemstone, lifting Al as though he were made of paper and slamming him against the shelves of pickled whatnot. He slid limply to the floor, accompanied by the music of tinkling glass and splashing preservative fluid. The blow to the head had him hearing something that sounded like feminine laughter. Creepy, maniacal laughter.

"Please let that be a hallucination from dain bramage, please be a hallucination from dain bramage," he murmured, opening his eyes. A pulsing purple light filled the shop. "Crap. That can't be good."

"Indeed," a voice agreed. "Come forth, that I may thank you for freeing me."

Al struggled to his feet and beheld a feminine form, constructed entirely of glowing crystals, standing amongst the wrecked shelves of the abandoned store. The entity stared into his soul with sapphire eyes, beckoning him with a clawed finger. It had no mouth, but he could hear its laughter nonetheless.

"Yeah, this is gonna suck," Al sighed. "Gotta stop touching everything."

"Wisdom often comes from a mistake," the crystalline creature stated. "I've been trapped in there for *ages*, and I'm so very hungry." It studied Al as though he were a juicy steak slathered in caramelized onions. "You will do for now."

Al thrust out his hand, pointing with his forefinger and pinky, and bellowed, "*Shocker!*" The lightning exploded from his fingertips and danced across the surface of her crystal hide. The energy sank into the hard gemstone and the being laughed.

"That whet my appetite nicely. Is that the best you can do?"

Thinking quickly, Al scooped up the cumbersome padlock and hurled it at her. As it sailed toward her, he drove his will at it, propelling it to greater speed. The metal smashed into her chest, glancing off with a *crack*. Chunks of her hide spalled off in all directions. The lock went spinning off to a corner of the shop, and Al staggered against the counter, drained from the exertion.

The being stared down at her chest. There, marring her former perfection, was a spiderweb of fissures. Her head came up and her eyes flashed with cerulean rage. "You'll pay for that."

"Yeah," Al snorted. "I get that a lot."

She thrust out her hand and a tsunami of power hammered Al. He was flung off his feet like a leaf on the wind and slammed into the already broken shelves. Glass from shattered reliquaries and jars pierced his back, and he cried out as the preservatives stung him like swarms of fire ants. He crumpled to the floor, reeling from the impact and the pain. Vaguely, he heard the creaking of overstressed timbers.

"Crap," he muttered, covering his head.

The shelves, pushed past their breaking point, collapsed. Al was buried beneath an avalanche of splintered wood, expired pickled things and random semiprecious gemstones. The shelves, of course, retained enough structural integrity to pin him beneath their splintery bulk.

He couldn't move, but he could see. The crystalline monster tore the counter from its moorings with contemptuous ease and flung it against the distant wall as though it were a child's ball. She stared down at him, and her evil mirth pealed throughout the shop once more.

"I shall enjoy draining you slowly," she told the trapped mage. "I will drain you until you are near death again and again, and you will feed me until you are utterly mad. Then, after I have conquered this world, when you no longer amuse me, I shall end your pathetic life."

"Sounds fun," Al told her, blinking against the blood running into his left eye. "But it'll never happen. You've forgotten something."

"Oh?" she snarled. "Going to throw another lock at me?"

"Always watch your back, dumbass."

Perplexed, the creature asked, "What?"

Skullcrusher's massive head impacted on the dead center of her upper back, where the spine would be located between the shoulder blades on a human. The crystalline entity collapsed to her knees with a cry of pained outrage. Slivers of crystal erupted from the rifts spiderwebbing across her back. Gorak hefted the hammer with an earsplitting war cry and brought the weapon of his ancestors down on her again. More crystal shards flew from her as her faceted hide cracked. Purplish mist began to leak from her wounds in dribbles and spurts.

She held up her hand to block an attack, and the arm shattered like glass beneath the assault. Gorak's hammer was everywhere, smashing against her from all angles, destroying her defenses. Somehow, the accursed troll was able to evade her attempts to force him back. She had never known such agony, or such fear.

With a scream, she surrounded herself with a dome of force. The war hammer struck her shield so savagely it nearly collapsed. Her eternity within the prison had left her weak, vulnerable to these fleshy beings and their primitive weapons. As the hammer rose, she turned the shield into a shockwave, knocking the enormous troll backwards. Somehow, the beast kept itself on its feet.

Wearily, her life force spilling from her multitude of injuries and the stump of her destroyed arm, she stood. "You, I will slay quickly," she informed the troll.

Stunningly, the creature chuckled happily. "Long has it been since I faced a worthy foe. I welcome your challenge, fiend."

He charged, feinting to her armless side. She lashed out with a focused beam of sheer power, but it only devastated the ruined shop further. Gorak stepped aside, spinning away and bringing the hammer to bear on her remaining arm. It exploded beneath the hammer's caress, barely depleting the weapon's momentum. Skullcrusher struck her side, cracking more of her façade and lifting her off her feet. She flew through the stale air of the shop, only to crash violently into the wall.

Disarmed, her life bleeding away from myriad rents in her hide, she struggled to rise. Gorak dashed to where she lay, a primal roar bursting from his tusked mouth. Skullcrusher whistled through the air as it bore down on her head with meteoric energy.

Her head shattered like a cheap vase, and she died. All of her remaining power burst from her in one apocalyptic blast. The wall of the abandoned shop suddenly developed a new door. The roof gained a new skylight. Gorak was flung off his feet, his leather armor tattered. The earth shook as he landed in a dazed and crumpled heap.

But the worst of the damage was suffered by Skullcrusher itself. The ancient weapon, carried by the scion of every generation of the troll's clan, had been protected from harm by a skillfully designed and mighty enchantment. Thousands of blows against steel armor and weapons had never scratched the war hammer.

The demise of the crystalline entity sundered the enchantment as though it were the clumsy work of a first-year apprentice. The matrix of spellwork defending the stone fractured, releasing all of the magic in a sympathetic detonation. Stone shattered, and Gorak was left clutching a broken stick.

As the troll sat up, he stared at the nightmare clenched in his fist. Skullcrusher had seen centuries of battle. The sweat and blood of dozens of his ancestors had stained the wooden handle. He had lost his place in his clan, the approval of his family, and now at the sunset of this terrible day, he was without his family's ancestral weapon. He had lost *everything*.

For the second time since he had become a warrior, and for the second time since this horrid day had begun, Gorak wept like a child.

Al, ever the sensitive sort, attempted to comfort his bereft companion. "That really sucks, dude. Can you dig me outta here?"

Chapter 20

The things dropping from the trees were so truly awful the mere sight of them made Inigo's eyes ache. They had tentacles, limbs of loricated plates, and far too many eyes. His mind refused to maintain a defined view of them, so they appeared to him as monsters which constantly altered their shapes and sizes. Jaws like those of a shark gnashed in anticipation and drool as thick as lamp oil ran between their serrated teeth.

The elf danced between them, hacking off tentacles and claws and drawing their attention from Hester, who was hurriedly dressing and getting to her feet. He had to buy her time enough to join the fight, or they would both be overwhelmed. Claws raked across his armor, damaging the fine ringmail. Inigo continued fighting, shocked by the ruination of the fine elven steel. His blades were smoking as the blood of the horrors pitted the metal like an acid bath.

He lashed out at a thing to his right, driving the dying steel into its middle. It squealed like a stuck pig and collapsed in a quivering pile at his feet. Its body immediately began to dissolve, exuding a foul-smelling black smoke as its acidic fluids devoured the corpse. Two more of the things raced to fill the gap in the line their fallen companion had left.

The sword in his left hand snapped off midway up the blade as he smashed it into a beast to his left. Furious, Inigo stabbed the horror behind him with the destroyed blade, leaving the remaining steel buried to the hilt in its flesh.

Dodging a thicket of flailing tentacles, the elf snatched up a thick tree branch. He thrust the makeshift wooden club into the maw of one monster and drove the tip of his sword between the eyes of another. Still more took their places. His remaining sword looked like a wooden toy beset by termites.

A lucky strike from a tentacle tripped him, and Inigo fell to his knees. He turned the fall into a roll, slashing at two of the damned things as he tumbled. He regained his feet, returning himself to a guarding stance. He held his sword before him, readying for the next attack, and the rotted blade fell apart with a wet *snap*. He tossed the remains of his expensive weapons at the horrors and prepared himself for the end.

From somewhere to his left, he heard the thud of wood against flesh. Firelight gleamed hungrily, and the creatures hissed in outrage. One of the beasts fled past Inigo, hissing madly as it trailed flaming bits of itself across the forest floor. Cursing vehemently, Hester waded into the fight, the Staff of Flameyness dealing death and fire.

The magical weapon had turned the tide of the battle, just as it had with the goblins. Inigo grimly strode into the fight again, smashing his club into the fleeing monstrosities until the dead wood broke into pieces too small to use as weapons.

When the last of the abominations had finally died or fled, the pair were much the worse for the wear. Inigo's armor had been shredded and eaten away. Some of his hair had been burned away, and his hands and arms were covered in lesions from the blood of the creatures. Hester's clothing had been utterly ruined, torn, devoured by acid, and burned. Like Inigo, her arms would bear the scars from droplets of their blood. Most annoyingly, the stupid things had eaten one of her shoes.

"I hate this stupid forest," Hester snarled as she stared down at one of the smoking puddles.

Inigo was inclined to agree. He had been raised to love the trees, to love nature, but this was one forest he never wished to see again. "We should move, before those things return."

"What were they?" Hester asked.

The elf shook his head. "I have no idea."

'They' were descendants of creatures summoned through a rift in reality by an ancient race of wizards known as Gineers. *The Adventurer's Almanac* discusses the wonders and horrors this amazing race once wrought in Chapter 239: *Lend me your Gineers*. This species, who were apparently very similar to humans, had astonishing control over the elements, and were capable of phenomenal metalwork and masonry. Their technology bordered on magical, and their control of magic far exceeded that of any other race — until they annihilated themselves. The Forest of Despair contained one of their many devastated cities, which had been overrun by extradimensional horrors, ancestors to those Inigo and Hester had encountered.

The human and elf gathered up their remaining supplies and resumed their journey. Sometimes they heard chittering and hissing from the trees above, but the horrors never renewed their assault. It had been centuries since anything had brought them pain and death, and their newfound mortality made them cautious.

When the sun began to rise, Inigo and Hester had reached the edge of the forest. They were on a ridge overlooking a valley that appeared to have been carved with a single swipe of some titan's soup spoon. There, surrounded by the ruins of a small stone fortress, was the black, gaping mouth of a cave.

A faded sign lounging beside the fort declared it to be 'n D'om'. The rest of the sign appeared to have been washed away by rains and faded by the blazing sun. A collection of skulls littered the ground in front of the sign. More skulls, mostly from horses and cattle, had been placed on poles and old spears around the entrance to the cave.

"Quite the welcoming façade," Inigo remarked. "Shall we?"

"Oh, yes," Hester replied, a savage grin twisting her features. "Let's find these bandits and root them out like the weeds they are."

The walk down the ridge was easy enough. The killing field before the fortress raised the elf's hackles a bit, but they faced no opposition. In a spate of poor planning on the part of the bandits, the fortress itself was deserted. An enormous wooden door barred entrance to the cavern of R'an D'om, but it was strangely unlocked.

Inigo opened the portal slowly, lifting it slightly to ensure its rusty hinges pivoted as quietly as possible. Nothing but the cool darkness of the cavern greeted them. They stepped inside, and Inigo closed it behind them.

The elf's eyes adjusted immediately to the dim torchlight within the cave. He saw no threats, no bandits and no cave-dwelling monsters eager to devour them. There was only the smooth, water-sculpted walls and floor of the cave, and a ceiling spiked with stalactites. Inigo led them deeper into the cave.

Chapter 21

The excursion into the haunted apothecary's shop had left Feather with a lead weight in her stomach. Al had been injured badly and nearly killed. Gorak's prized war hammer had been destroyed. The shop itself was utterly wrecked. The only member of their group who had been useless in the fight had emerged totally unscathed, and Joel's cruel worlds echoed in her head.

Worst of all, nothing in the shop had proven worth the risk. The crystalline monster had destroyed nearly everything, and had been reduced to a few bags of, probably, worthless gemstones. The few items in the store's inventory which hadn't been expired had been ruined in the explosion. Upon further inspection, the baubles Al had discovered were worthless fakes.

After Gorak had finished mourning his loss, he had shoved the broken shelves off Al's back. Then, the group had fled into the night before the guards could arrive to inspect the devastation. More work for the guards, especially the captain, weighed on Feather's conscience as well.

"I think I'm cursed," she muttered as they settled for the night in Jeremy's home.

"No," Gorak disagreed, sprawling out on the floor near the hearth. His ruined leather tunic made a passable pillow. "If anyone among us is cursed, it is I."

"No one's cursed," Al said, waving off their lamentations. "Shit happens. Sometimes it sucks. Sometimes it don't. Either way, none of it's from some crazy curse or whatever."

"Do wizards not cast curses?" Gorak demanded hotly. "Do gypsies not cast curses? Are there not cursed artifacts?"

Al considered this for a moment. "Well, I meant in general."

"Sprites are taught that everything we do comes back to us," Feather countered. "Our actions can very well curse us."

"Not the point," Al replied. "And it ain't like you've ever done anything worthy of being cursed, Feather. Me, on the other hand… I've made a mess of things today. And yesterday. And for pretty much my entire life.

"Hell's bells, I got Gorak's friend killed. Didn't mean to, but that's how it is. I feel terrible about it, but I ain't about to sit around here lamenting and stewing in guilt over something I didn't intend to happen."

"Mage," Gorak grunted, "shut your mouth. I do not wish to be reminded of my failure to defend him. Had I been vigilant, I might've seen the blade coming. My distraction cost him his life."

"Fair enough," Al relented miserably. "New subject, then."

"No," the troll growled. "Sleep. We will part in the morning, and never speak on this matter again."

"I think we should stay together," Feather blurted. Both mage and troll stared at her. "If I hadn't seen that spirit, Al wouldn't have gotten hurt, and Gorak wouldn't have lost his hammer. I owe you both a debt. If we part, I won't be able to live with myself."

The troll laid his head back down. "In the morning, we will speak further, *rusgol*." *Rusgol* was the troll word for 'little warrior'. "For now, rest."

Al spent the night in the dead angler's chair, drinking the murdered man's wine. Long after the troll had begun to snore and the sprite had fallen asleep with her head leaning against Renato's furry side, the mage remained wakeful. Al was somewhat bemused to discover that opossums also snored. He couldn't sleep until the boozy oblivion finally conquered his guilt and demons.

Morning came with a skull-splitting headache. Al clambered out of the chair, stretching his sore and bruised back. The troll and the sprite were gone, and he had a momentary bout of panic at being alone in this strange house. Then, he noticed their armor lying empty on the floor. Renato the opossum glared up at him, sizing him up. Al took a step forward, and the jack bared his teeth and hissed a warning.

"Good morning to you too, jerk," the wizard spat. "Anything to eat around here?" The opossum hissed as if in answer, and Al snorted, "I mean, besides garbage, you disgusting freak."

A shadow moved in front of the back window, and Al staggered over to peer outside. "Well, don't see that every day."

In the garden out back, the troll stood in a crouch, his arms positioned as though fighting an opponent only he could see. To his left, the sprite mimicked his stance. Gorak stepped forward, keeping his stance steady, and lashed out with his left hand in a punch, following with a strike from his left elbow. Feather did the same.

As Al looked on, the massive troll gracefully fended off opponents to all the cardinal directions, returning to the center between each movement. Then, he assaulted foes to the northeast, the southwest, the northwest and the southeast. Every motion was strong and smooth as silk, the result of decades of rigorous practice.

Feather mirrored his motions very well for a novice, occasionally stumbling or flubbing a move. The troll would halt, mid-stride, and patiently allow her to correct her stance or position. Under his gentle tutelage, the sprite rapidly improved until she was almost as proficient as her instructor. Then, Gorak would lead her through the routine a bit faster, sometimes adding more complex motions, until both of them were dripping with sweat.

They ended the training with slight bows to each other, before coming inside. Gorak's chest, Al noted, was a patchwork of scars. The troll bore these signs of battle proudly, smiling as he noticed the mage's rather impolite stare. Feather arched one shapely eyebrow at Al.

"Never seen a scar before?" she asked.

"Not that many on one man," Al replied, a bit in awe. "Thought trolls had pretty tough hides."

Gorak laughed, shaking the rafters. "We do. The foes who scarred me would've easily slain a mere human. We are not, however, invincible. Blades and claws can still injure us."

Feather stretched, arching her back. Al's eyes immediately took in the small breasts straining against the fabric of her rough tunic. The sprite's wings fluttered a few times, and Feather straightened. Catching Al's gaze, she snorted, "Forget it, human. You are not my type."

Blushing, Al averted his gaze. "Sorry. You're kinda pretty."

"'Kinda'?" Feather snarled hotly. "I'll have you know that I am one of the best looking females in my clan, you ass. And you're not exactly a paragon of masculine beauty yourself, you know."

Gorak intervened before Al's mouth could draw in his hoof again. "Enough. I'm sure both of you are attractive enough to members of your own species. Now, if you've completed your bickering, I must go to the undertaker and see that my friend is properly buried."

"I'll go with you," Feather declared. "No one should bury a friend alone."

"I've got nothing better to do," Al stated. "I'll come, too."

The troll frowned. "We agreed to part this morning. I will go alone. Neither of you knew Jeremy."

Feather hurriedly began to don her armor, pointedly ignoring Al's stares. "I never agreed to that," she countered.

"Very well," Gorak sighed. "I suppose I should welcome your company. As soon as you are ready, we shall go."

Al was a little hurt. "What about me?" he whined. "We make a good team, Gorak. I spell things, you smash things."

The troll's square jaw dropped. "Are you mad, human? You were nearly slain by that crystal monster. My clan's most valuable weapon was destroyed. We laid waste to a shop. In what reality were we a 'good team'?"

The wizard grinned. "Never heard of crystalline entities before, have you? The last time anyone fought one of those monsters, it wiped out an entire *army*. I walked out of there with a few bruises and cuts. You walked out without a single scratch. I'd say that qualifies as 'good', wouldn't you?"

The troll was skeptical, but he assumed the wizard would know more of magical beings than himself. "I will take you at your word, human. We will remain together, for now."

After Feather had donned her armor, the group left the dead man's house. Gorak's heart was a lead weight in his broad chest, and his pensive silence settled over them all like a dark blanket soaked in urine. They plodded down the streets, headed north toward the mortuary. Other pedestrians parted before them like cheap curtains, though whether they were avoiding the frowning troll or the hissing opossum was anyone's guess.

The mortuary was an oddly cheerful building, Al thought. It was all gleaming white stone, trimmed with bright greens. Beautiful flowers bloomed around its doors and beneath its wide, inviting windows. The trees planted around the sprawling building were well-trimmed and sighed pleasantly in the breeze. The building itself seemed to exude peace, inspiring serenity, and Al opened his mind's eye to investigate.

Outlined brilliantly on the stone were glowing blue runes. The entire building was covered in spellwork aimed at calming and comforting every living thing within a block of the mortuary. It was an impressive enchantment, and Al's mind boggled at the expense the undertaker must have incurred for this benevolent magic. The mage immediately liked this mortician.

Feather also saw the arcane runes and instantly grasped their intent. "Amazing," she whispered. "This human must truly care about his customers."

"It is not unpleasant," Gorak muttered. He was feeling a bit better since arriving at the mortuary, but he found it strange. The pain of his failure was still with him, but it was muted, muffled somehow. This place was almost as peaceful as the lakeside with a fishing pole in his hand.

They entered the mortuary's front door. Above them, a bell tinkled cheerfully. The lobby was tastefully decorated with elegantly made furniture and relaxing paintings. The hardwood floor had been polished to a dark, lustrous shine. Double doors led to the right and left, and a well-dressed man with a neat beard and a sympathetic expression entered the lobby from the right.

"Good morning," he said in a voice that was almost musical. "You are Gorak, Jeremy's friend," he said, addressing the troll. "He was a good and kind man, and our community is diminished for his loss."

Gorak nodded. "I thank you for your words. I have come to see to arrangements for him."

The mortician smiled sadly. "All of this has been taken care of, Gorak. Jeremy came to me when he was diagnosed with the cancer. His funeral costs have been paid, and everything he wanted is ready to be carried out as soon as my work preparing his body is completed. Would you like to see him?"

"No," Gorak replied. "He is no longer there. I have brought this," he held up Skullcrusher's shattered handle, "to be buried with him. It is tradition amongst my people, that they be interred with the remains of a weapon which has seen honorable combat. A fallen weapon for a fallen man."

The undertaker nodded and accepted the ruined handle reverently. "I will ensure this request is fulfilled. In two days, your friend's body will be ready. I… There is no way to say this delicately, but Jeremy had no family remaining in Gunnar's Rest, and we do not know where his son has gone. As such, we have been unable to arrange pallbearers."

The troll inclined his head. "I will carry him."

"The casket will be heavy," the mortician stated. "Loaded, it will weigh at least four hundred pounds."

Gorak smiled grimly. "I shall carry him. Has his grave been excavated?"

"Oh, yes. All arrangements have been made, and I have personally checked to ensure that the grave is of the proper size. Is there anything else I can do for you, Gorak?"

"I think not," the troll replied softly. "See to my friend. I will return in two days."

Once outside the mortuary, Gorak turned to Al. "Can you find him?"

Al blinked. "Nissan?" The troll simply stared, and the wizard muttered, "Who else? Look, it's not that simple, Gorak. I can't just wave my hands and have the magic locate him. I need something of his to do a locator spell. A hair, some clothes, a few drops of blood… I've got none of that."

"Then we shall have to rely upon the guards," the troll muttered. "We need to speak to Captain Phil McCracken and see what his investigation has found."

Chapter 22

Inigo and Hester hadn't gone far when they reached a fork in the cave. The branch to the right sloped downward, ending at a wooden door banded with black iron. The way to their left climbed slightly but was blocked by an iron gate. Thin rivulets of water trickled through the black bars, running downhill to merge into a single small stream which flowed steadily under the wooden door.

"Which way?" Hester asked.

"Left, I think," Inigo said. "The gate appears more difficult to breach, so it stands to reason that the valuables Joel deposited in this place would be stored behind it. Also, with the waters flowing under the door, that side may flood."

The elf strode to the gate, examining its corroded hinges. He gripped the bars and pulled, but the gate refused to move. The lock was broken and hung open like a yokel's gaping piehole, but the ancient hinges were frozen with rust. He tugged harder, and the anchors driven into the stone wall of the cavern twitched slightly. He placed his boot alongside the topmost anchor and yanked.

There was a screech of tortured metal, and the weakened iron anchor released its grip on the rock. He twisted the heavy gate, and the lower anchor snapped off. After a bit of shoving and grunting, the way was clear, and he removed one of the torches flanking the door from its sconce.

They hadn't gone far when Inigo's keen ears heard shuffling footsteps. There was someone heading their way, but they sounded as though they had been injured. Their gait was unsteady, like one of their legs was broken. Then, Inigo caught the scent of decay.

"Undead," he growled, wishing he still had his swords. He hefted the torch like a club, and warned Hester to be ready.

A corpse staggered into the light from Inigo's torch. Once, it had been a large man, dressed in leather armor. Death had shriveled him, and the moisture of the cavern had reduced his armor to moldy tatters which clung to the rotting corpse like tattered strands of seaweed. The walking corpse stared at them through grayish cataracts, moans spilling over its peeling lips. A hand reached toward them, skin dangling beneath exposed muscle as its teeth gnashed hungrily.

"It smells awful," Hester complained, pinching her nostrils shut. "Would you kill that stupid thing already?"

The elf bit back his first response. Instead of reminding her that he was without an appropriate weapon, he decided to improvise. Inigo dashed up the wall to his right, springing off the stone. He grabbed one of the stalactites, snapping it off near the ceiling before he dropped to the ground.

Hundreds of years of water dripping had formed a tooth of stone that tapered to a wicked point. Inigo drove the tip of the rock through the zombie's temple, destroying its brain. It collapsed like a marionette with its strings severed, and Inigo abruptly withdrew the makeshift weapon.

"Crude, but effective," he chuckled.

"It smells awful," Hester griped again, as though Inigo hadn't heard her the first time. She jabbed it with the Staff of Flameyness, and the magical weapons ignited the putrescent flesh. Rancid fat and skin burned with an eerie green light, and the corpse began to sizzle and pop beneath the flame's kiss. The acrid smoke was preferable to the stench of rotting flesh, but only slightly. The illumination, on the other hand, far surpassed the meager light from Inigo's torch.

The elf cringed. The entire passage was lined with bodies. Corpses littered the floor, lounged against the sloping walls of the cavern, and even hung from the ceiling. None of them were moving, but the undead were known to hibernate when food was unavailable. While in that state, they were indistinguishable from a normal carcass, and they could wait until Inigo or Hester was within their grasp before they struck.

It was a fiendish trap, and Inigo was compelled to grudgingly respect its implementation. The zombies would wait to strike, falling upon intruders. The intruders would feed the undead, and be turned themselves, and the zombies would return to their hibernation, ready to spring the trap again.

Crouching, he tore the left arm from the burning corpse. He held the limb over the flames, turning it into a grotesque torch. When the arm was burning brightly, he tossed it into the midst of the corpses further along the passageway.

The severed limb bounced across the bodies, leaving a trail of flaming flesh. Quickly, the blaze spread to the corpses, and the results were dramatic. The flaming corpses sprung to life, flailing their burning limbs as they struggled to rise. They staggered against other slumbering zombies, spreading the fire until the entire cavern was filled with the conflagration.

A wave of foul-smelling heat washed over Inigo as the horde collectively rushed to eat the intruders. Inigo's testicles drew up against his body as his gross miscalculation dawned upon him. The fire wouldn't destroy the undead before he and Hester were overrun.

"We should run!" he blurted, heeding his own advice.

The pair dashed for the cave's mouth, and fiery Hell shambled after them. At the fork, Inigo sent Hester on ahead, while he stayed and pounded frantically on the iron-reinforced wooden door. On the other side, he heard someone talking, and footsteps approaching. Grinning, the elf continued to pound on the wood until the burning undead were within grappling distance, before fleeing after Hester.

Behind him, he heard the door swing open. There was a distressed man's shout, and the groans of the undead reached a fever pitch. The elf never looked back, and continued sprinting for the exit, the length of stalactite still clamped in his right hand.

Chapter 23

Captain Phil McCracken needed a full night's rest and a shave. Over the past two days, he'd dealt with muggings, robberies, wife beatings, horse theft, arson, murder, the destruction of an abandoned shop, and a barroom brawl. The latter four incidents all directly involved one or more of the three individuals standing in his office.

Life had gotten really interesting in his town, and it could all be laid on that asshole Joel's stupid summons. Gunnar's Rest had been flooded by adventurers, vagabonds, ne'er-do-wells, treasure hunters and other random idiots, and his guards were running themselves ragged trying to keep up. The trio of people in front of his desk weren't making the job any easier.

"What in the Nine Blue Hells were you thinking?" McCracken demanded, all pretense of civility evaporating like spit on a griddle. "Assaulting Joel, wrecking the old apothecary shop… Are you three dolts trying to give me an ulcer?"

"No," Gorak replied coolly. "We were attempting to get a job from Joel. He was *uncivil*."

McCracken snorted at the troll's summation. "Yeah, he's a pain in the keister. You stepped in it this time,

Gorak. That wizard wants your head on a pike, and I don't know that I can protect you from all of the other imbeciles he's called into town. I've told him I don't want vigilante bullshit on my streets, but wizards don't tend to listen all that well." The captain stared meaningfully at Al as he said this.

"Now, care to tell me what the blazes you were thinking when you wrecked up the old apothecary shop? Where did you dipshits get a damn bomb, anyway?"

"It was my fault," Feather responded, gazing at the floor. "I saw a ghost inside the shop. It was guarding a crystal monster that attacked Al. Gorak killed it, and it exploded, destroying the building and Gorak's hammer."

McCracken pinched the bridge of his nose. "Let me get this straight: you three fought a ghost and a crystal thing, and the crystal thing wrecked the shop? My boots ain't tall enough to wade through this horseshit."

"It's the truth!" Al exclaimed. He held up the bagged remains of the crystalline entity. "Here's what's left of the entity."

The captain of the guard peered into the burlap sack, seeing only shards of worthless gems. "Right. And why were you trespassing in the shop to begin with?"

"There was a ghost," Al replied. "We went in to investigate."

"Which wasn't your damn job!" McCracken snapped, slamming a fist down on the desktop. "That's the second building in two days, asshole! Granted, the Boarskull needed to be razed to the ground, and the shop was abandoned, but you're sowing chaos on my streets. Give me one reason not to have you flogged."

"Uh, Cap, what do you think would've happened if it had been someone else who entered that shop?" Al inquired cautiously. "I mean, eventually the town would've hired someone to tear the place down, right? Or tried to sell it?"

"I suppose," McCracken allowed. He had an idea as to where the mage was going with this.

"Right," Al continued. "And what do you think would've happened if someone uninitiated had awakened that entity? The last time in recorded history that some non-magical people went up against one of those things, it wiped out an entire *army*."

The guard captain clenched his jaw. He wasn't sure if the wizard was telling the truth, but he couldn't necessarily discount the assessment either. If Al was right, he had prevented greater carnage.

Al pressed the advantage. "You know I'm right, Cap. Feather, me, and Gorak kept the town safe from that thing. We deserve a reward, not a flogging."

McCracken sighed. "How about I withhold the public flogging for now, provided you dumbasses don't wreck anything else without my say so? For now, I'll tell the council that you cleaned out the shop on my orders and that it just went sideways. Don't do anything else without talking to me first. We sanguine?"

"Perfectly, Cap," Al replied cheerfully.

"Uh huh. Gorak, we haven't been able to find this Nissan character who murdered Jeremy. Unlike you three, he's kept a low profile. No one matching his description has left town, and my guards haven't seen him. None of our usual informants have reported seeing him. Not much to go on, I'm afraid."

"I will find him," Gorak snarled.

The captain glared at the troll. "No, you won't. I won't have civilians roaming my streets, causing problems. Only my guards are carrying out police actions in my town. That's how the council wants it."

The troll met the captain's gaze. "You cannot stop me, now that you have failed. The killer must not be allowed to get away with this."

McCracken sighed. "You're not listening. Only *my guards* are carrying out police actions in my town."

Gorak was about to bellow something at the captain when Feather perked up. "We'll take that job you offered, Captain."

The troll glanced at the sprite. He'd forgotten about the captain's offer to join the guards, and he hadn't realized that Feather had received the same offer. He would be able to hunt his friend's killer, and the captain would be able to assuage the council. The little sprite was proving her worth.

"Welcome to the guards!" McCracken boomed. He reached into a drawer and tossed a pair of badges on his desk. "You'll be our contingent's first troll and sprite." He looked at Al and frowned. "You can be attached to them as a civilian consultant, I reckon."

Al grinned. "I've never been a civilian consultant before! Or any other kind of consultant. Do I get a badge, too?"

"No. But you also don't get stripes on your mangy hide," McCracken replied coldly. "Now, all of you, get the Hell outta my office!"

Chapter 24

The smoke rolling out of the Cave of R'an D'om finally began to taper off around noon. The stench of smoldering rancid flesh, on the other hand, would probably linger in the valley for days. Inigo and Hester had settled themselves a fair distance away from the mouth of the cave, but still within the ruined fortress. They were snacking on some of Hester's supplies, Inigo's having been lost somewhere on the Jane Plain, when one of the bandits stumbled out into the fresh air.

He was doubled over, wracked by a coughing fit. His piecemeal armor was smeared with gore and stained with soot. After a few moments, he stood and spat a wad of black phlegm onto the grass. He gazed upward, his reddened eyes searching the heavens. A battered and nicked scimitar dangled limply from his right hand. He turned toward the alcove in which Hester and Inigo had enjoyed their lunch and his eyes widened in shock as Inigo drove a spear through his throat.

Gurgling and bleeding, the bandit fell to his knees, grasping at the length of oak jutting from his neck. He flopped to the ground, his eyes beginning to glaze, and the elf ripped the weathered weapon free. Inigo quickly searched the dying man, finding a bag of random coins and a poorly forged dagger. Between the sword and the dagger, the elf was armed, albeit with lousy weapons.

"My thanks, friend," he muttered to the corpse. Then, noticing a bite wound on the bandit's left arm, he drove the spear tip through the dead human's skull. The rotted wood snapped under the impact, leaving over a foot of shaft protruding from the head. The elf tossed the broken weapon aside and led Hester back into the cavern.

The stink was overpowering, and Inigo's stomach churned violently. But the air was breathable, and the stench meant that there would be fewer zombies with which to contend. They came to the fork, which was layered with smoldering corpses. None of the bodies moved or reacted to their presence as they stepped over, and often, on the carcasses. The cleansing fire had proven most effective.

The Adventurer's Almanac discusses zombies and other reanimated corpses at length in Chapter 124: *Fundead!* According to our research, the quickest, most effective way to eliminate a zombie is by destroying the brain. We do *not* recommend setting them on fire. Zombies will often burn quite well, and fire will eventually destroy them, but having a flaming corpse flailing about is hardly optimal. Attempting to destroy undead with fire has, in fact, resulted in mass destruction of property, particularly in areas comprised primarily of wooden structures.

For example, the village of Knobbly Bottom was once besieged by several dozen zombies. One of the town's defenders doused the horde with lamp oil and shot them with a flaming arrow. The undead were immediately engulfed in an inferno. The heat of the blaze drove the defenders back, allowing the zombies to swarm into the village. The resulting fire saw the destruction of the town's entire grain supply, the town hall and the chapel, as well as all but four of the houses.

The townspeople were forced to flee to neighboring villages, as winter was coming. The necromancer behind the attack was quoted as saying, "That was *awesome*! Those nose-picking villagers did all the work for me!" when our researchers visited him at his castle where the village had once stood. He now rules over the entire valley from his throne made of skulls, and produces a highly profitable line of scented candles, aimed at the occultist who really prefers his spells to smell better than the chicken he is sacrificing.

In any case, the flaming zombies (not to be confused with The Flamin' Zombies, a popular minstrel group) had utterly wiped out the bandits inhabiting the Cave of R'an D'om. Inigo and Hester encountered no resistance at all in the right branch of the cavern.

"Almost wasn't a challenge," Inigo opined cheerfully. The chamber in which the bandits had set up shop was big enough to hold several herds of elephants, and ringed with chests and barrels of loot. A far corner reeked like a latrine. There were even tables and crudely fashioned beds for at least a dozen men.

"Shall we search the crates, chests and barrels?" he asked Hester.

She responded with a fierce grin, loaded with avarice. "Most definitely. Joel said we'd know what was his when we saw it. Let's go smash some things!"

An hour later, they had broken into the last barrel, opened the last chest, and cracked the last crate. The barrels were all filled with food, mostly salted fish and pork. The crates were stuffed with assorted crap, primarily clothes and cooking utensils. Coins of silver, gold and copper spilled from a few of the chests, but the majority were empty. Looting the corpses had produced a quiver of cheaply made arrows, several daggers, a hand axe and some swords in deplorable condition.

Smashing an empty crate in frustration, Inigo groused, "If Joel stored anything of value in this chamber, the bandits must've sold it. We should search the rest of the cave."

They passed through the ruined iron gate and followed the narrow corridor until it ended at a heavily made door. This portal was constructed of thick timbers, bolted together, and clad in plates of steel. A series of locks held it securely shut. Strange glowing symbols had been carved into the steel, and the mere sight of them made Hester shudder.

"I don't like this door," she told Inigo. "Whoever carved those runes into the metal was extremely powerful. I think we should leave it alone and return to Joel. He can come open this door himself."

"What do you see?" Inigo inquired. He saw nothing but a steel-clad door. "I don't see anything, so you'll have to be my eyes."

Stepping closer, Hester stared at the runes. The nearer she drew, the deeper a reddish purple they glowed. She could feel them pulsing with power, sending waves of energy over her skin. Her hair began to stand on end, as though lightning had crashed near her. She reached out her left hand, hovering just a hairsbreadth from the surface of the door. A cold tingle walked its way up her arm, as though someone had begun jabbing her skin with sharp icicles. She could feel the power coursing over her, yet she was drawn to it like a moth to a flame.

She was about to touch the door when Inigo grabbed her wrist. "I do not believe you should do that," he stated. "I could feel the electricity in the air, like the air during a thunderstorm. I've seen what lightning can do to the mightiest of trees, and I would prefer that you not share their fate."

Hester looked at him and smiled. "You've never seen me ride the lightning."

She shook him off and slammed her palm on the door. The world washed out in a flash of blue and red. There was only Hester and the enchantment on the door. She pushed her consciousness into the steel and wood and was startled to encounter another mind.

Who are you? the voice demanded.

"I am Hester, emissary of Joel. We are here to reclaim Joel's crap," Hester replied. "Will you open the door?"

How do I know you really work for Joel?

Hester opened her consciousness to the voice. There was a slithering intrusion, a freezing cold snake driven into her brain. In her mind's eye, she saw her encounter with Joel replay in her mind, felt the mirth as the owner of the voice watched her memories.

You speak the truth. You may enter, if you dare. But I wouldn't recommend it.

"Why not?"

Joel didn't warn you about the guardian, did he?

Hester responded, "No. Joel didn't mention the zombies, either. What sort of 'guardian'?"

You should be wearing asbestos undergarments.

"What? Asbestos?"

The voice chuckled deeply at its joke. *Trust me, you don't want to go in there without asbestos underwear.*

And just like that, the link was broken. The locks snapped open with a series of clicks. Hester glanced at the elf. "The door says we need asbestos underwear."

Inigo was utterly baffled. "Asbestos? I don't understand. Why would we need... Asbestos is fatal."

Indeed, it can be. As noted in *The Adventurer's Almanac*, Chapter 180: *Stuff That'll Kill You!*, asbestos fibers lead to all sorts of maladies of the lungs, and these will eventually kill anyone unfortunate enough to inhale the fibers. Despite these dangers, asbestos is commonly used in applications involving fire and extreme heat, because asbestos is completely nonflammable.

And as the door had jokingly implied, nonflammable clothing would've been handy against the guardian of the chamber, a fact which became glaringly obvious to Inigo and Hester as they shoved open the door — coming face to face with a sleeping dragon.

The dragon itself was a rippled ebony and crimson. Its four wings were folded across its back. The great tail curled around its body was tipped with a spiked ball. A horned frill spread behind its massive head.

"Step back quietly," Inigo whispered. Hester nodded, her mouth frozen open in terror. They were about to retreat when the door slammed shut with a resounding *wham*! The pair stood, rooted to the spot. An amber eye the size of a dinner plate sprang open.

The head raised slowly, and the reptilian lips drew back in a snarl. Teeth the size of Inigo's pilfered dagger lined the enormous mouth. The beast's eyes narrowed, the jaws gaped and fluid filled the back of the throat. As Hester watched, the ball of ooze began to smolder. The dragon drew its head back and it horked the wad of smoking phlegm at the intruders. Right after leaving the maw, the dragon spit ignited, bursting into yellow-green flames.

Eyes wide, Hester was paralyzed by fear. Inigo, sensing her hesitation, shoved her aside and dove on top of her. The burning ball of dragon snot splattered all over the enchanted door, blocking the way. Infuriated, the dragon roared and lashed out with its tail. Inigo rolled Hester to the side, and the armored tail smashed into the stone floor, spraying them with rock chips.

The duo were on their feet and running when the next wad of flaming snot struck the spot where they had been laying. They fled deeper into the chamber, dodging dragon fire and stalagmites until they reached the end of the chamber. Hester and Inigo stood in a round alcove, surrounded by riches and artifacts.

"You cannot posssssibly hope to essssscape," the dragon hissed. "Come out of there, and I will make your end quick. Irritate me further, and you will die begging me for mercccy."

"Well, with an attitude like that, no wonder you have so many friends!" Hester snarled. "I killed a hydra on my own. I'm not about to be intimidated by some overgrown lizard!"

The dragon peered into their hole and chuckled, a sound like pebbles tumbling down a rocky slope. "Hydrassss are pathetic little wormsss compared to one sssuch asss me. You will die, one way or another."

"I notice you're not spitting your flaming mucus into this room," Inigo stated. "Could it be that you are forbidden from damaging its contents?"

After a brief hesitation, the dragon admitted, "Perhapsss."

Inigo scooped up a fragile-looking vase, noting with satisfaction the way the dragon's catlike pupil narrowed to focus on the pottery. "As guardian, it is your duty to protect these artifacts from harm, is it not?"

The dragon growled, "Maybe."

The elf smiled and dashed the vase to the floor. The dragon's eye widened as the pottery shattered into a million fragments, spilling some sort of powder. "Good," Inigo snapped. "I see I have your attention." He snatched up another vase. "I will personally destroy everything in this place before I die. You will have failed to protect Joel's treasure trove."

"You will die!" the dragon protested, its reptilian face drawn into a rictus of disbelief.

Inigo nodded. "Indeed. But you will still be a failure. Or you allow us to remove the items Joel sent us to collect, and continue your stewardship."

The dragon hissed in frustration. "Had that infernal door done itsss job, you never would've gotten passsst me."

"That's probably true," Inigo allowed. "But here we are. Do you accept my bargain?"

"Yessss. Take what Joel wanted. I will continue to watch over the remainder."

The elf looked to Hester. "Now, we need only determine what Joel intended for us to retrieve. Do you detect any magic within these artifacts?"

"Yeah, I do," she replied.

"Which ones?"

Hester sighed. "All of them. They're all enchanted, and I have no idea which ones Joel will want, because they're all high level enchantments."

The dragon laughed so loudly Hester's head ached. "You came in here with no clue what you were looking for? *Ha*! You're complete foolssss!"

"Says the 'guardian' who was asleep on the job," Inigo huffed.

"You have any idea how long I've been locked in thissss cave?" the dragon snarled. "You try ssstaying in here for a few centuriesss!"

"How did you get in here, anyway?" Hester asked. "There's no way you fit through that door, and I don't see any other way into this chamber."

"Been here my whole life," the dragon lamented. "Hatched here, grew up here, and I'll die here. Alone. In the dark."

Hester felt a moment of pity for the titanic black dragon. To have spent every day of his long life in this cavern, locked behind a door? It was an abomination. Joel was cruel beyond belief to have prevented this magnificent creature from ever having known the sky.

"What if we could set you free?" she asked. "You've never seen the sun or felt the wind beneath your wings. What if we could find a way to get you out of here?"

The dragon stared at her. "It cannot be done." He cocked his head skyward, revealing an odd collar around the base of his head. "Even if you could widen the corridor enough to permit me to leave, my collar would kill me the moment I departed. I can never leave. Take what you will and go."

Inigo and Hester each collected a few items from Joel's secret stash. They walked past the dragon, which was curling back up to resume its snooze. The door swung open of its own accord, and Hester could feel its disappointment. The door had been hoping the dragon would roast them, she realized.

Chapter 25

"I don't know anything!" the pickpocket shrieked. "I'm gonna hurl, dude! Put me down, please!"

Feather rolled her eyes. "I think he might be telling the truth, Gorak. Maybe you should let him go. Before he pukes, this time."

The troll had one beefy arm extended, holding the footpad in the air by the ankles. Everything had fallen out of the little thief's pockets and he had turned an unusual shade of purple, but he hadn't confessed to anything except petty theft. He appeared to know nothing of Nissan's whereabouts.

Gorak snorted. "Perhaps we should slay him anyway. He is, after all, a thief. It would be so simple to smash him repeatedly against the wall until he dies."

The thief's eyes widened. "What? You can't kill me for that! Why won't anyone help me? Help!"

Gorak rapped the pickpocket's head smartly against the cobblestones. "Stop your caterwauling, human. No one will help you. Who would know where Nissan is hiding?"

"I don't know!" he cried. "I don't even know who that guy is, dude! I'm gonna barf... *Hurk!*"

The stream of vomit narrowly missed the troll's feet. Disgusted, Gorak flung the thief away. The smaller man crashed into a pile of refuse, puking several more times into the rotten garbage. Infuriated beyond belief, Gorak stormed over to the footpad and placed one foot heavily on his back.

"Who?" Gorak snarled, shoving the man's face into a rotten zucchini. He let the sputtering man up just enough so that he could breathe, before cramming him back into the trash.

"O, I might know a guy!" the thief wailed, spitting out a mouthful of rancid squash. "He's got his fingers in everything. If this Nissan dude needed someone to hide him, Bricktop will know."

"Where is he?" the troll asked.

"Bricktop hangs out at The Gilded Truffle. He's a big dude, always dresses snazzy. Lots of gold rings and chains. You can't miss him."

"For your sake, human, you had better be telling the truth. If not, I will find you," Gorak warned, "and you will not enjoy our reunion."

As the footpad dashed off into the streets, Al remarked, "Gorak, you have a way with informants that'd be the envy of every guard in Canabeer — if it were legal."

"I am unconcerned with legality," Gorak replied evenly. "We will find this Bricktop, and he will give us Nissan."

"Where is this Gilded Truffle place?" Feather asked Al.

The mage was flummoxed for a moment. *See one reasonably attractive woman out of her armor, and my tongue quits working,* he thought. "Uh, lemme check the map I swiped from the Chamber of Commerce."

Al unfolded the map, which was easily the size of a tablecloth. Fortunately, all of the places of business were thoughtfully designated in Carolyn's pretentiously flowing script. He quickly scanned the map, finding a squarish blotch on the map, just a few blocks from where they stood. It was labeled 'The Gilded Truffle', and marked with a frowny face to indicate Carolyn's displeasure with the business in question. Al cheerfully noted that the unlamented Boarskull was marked with three of the scowling faces.

Clumsily refolding the map, Al crammed the wadded parchment back into his pocket. He pointed generally to the east. "Looks like it's that way. Carolyn doesn't like the place, so this should be interesting."

The walk to the squat brick building was pleasant enough, if one didn't mind traipsing along beside several hundred pounds of enraged, vengeance-fueled troll and disgruntled opossum. Al, naturally, was oblivious to the stomping, grumbling troll and the randomly hissing marsupial. He smiled, reveling in the beautiful blue, cloud-dappled sky and the gentle breeze ruffling his hair. Despite the reason for the stroll, the soreness of his back and the occasional sharp cobblestone stabbing his sort of bare feet, he found himself grinning like a happy village idiot.

The Gilded Truffle was an ugly building, a mishmash of designs that would've looked lovely on their own, but had been slammed together by some schizophrenic architect on a full moon. Worse, it had been painted an eye-gougingly hideous combination of greens, browns and gold that Al had last seen in fluffy rugs his parents had owned. The fact that anyone willingly built the monstrosity before him told Al that there had been a lot of psychedelic drugs involved. Which, come to think of it, was why his parents had bought that terrifying rug. In any case, the current owner was either colorblind, or just honestly didn't give a flying rat's ass that the property's hue had been inspired by mushrooms and vomit.

A bald, dark-skinned human in a fine suit stood by the wide front door, shielded from the sun by a pyramidal awning. He was almost as wide as Gorak, though at least three feet shorter, and wore a sword in an exquisitely crafted scabbard at his left hip. He stoically gazed out into the street, regarding the world with a practiced boredom. Two more men of similar build and fashion sense stood guard over the corners of the Truffle.

Gorak stomped right up to the guard and spitted him with a stare that would've sent lesser men scurrying for cover. The human tilted his head just enough to turn his terminally unimpressed stare upon the troll. "Name?"

"I am Gorak Stonecrusher," Gorak replied. "Guard in the employ of Captain Phil McCracken. We are here to speak to the one known as Bricktop."

The doorman cracked a sly smile. "You're not on the list. If you're not on the list, you don't see Mr Bricktop. Piss off."

Feather rode up to the wide man's ankles. "Sir, we're looking for a murderer. We were told Bricktop might be able to help."

He gazed down at the sprite and grimaced at Renato's hiss. "Is that a possum?"

"*O*possum, actually," she answered brightly. "Possums are very different animals. Now, could you please let us in?"

"Bricktop doesn't allow any animals in his club, miss. And if you're not on the list, you don't get in. None of you are on the list, so you're not getting in."

Sensing that Gorak was about to rip the doorman apart like a chicken, Al blurted, "Uh, Joel sent us."

The big man snorted. "No, he didn't. Bricktop doesn't do business with that pompous jackass. You three, and your weird pet, need to step off."

Gorak was out of patience. "You will move aside, human, or I will move you."

The guard laughed. "Do you have any idea who my boss is? Bricktop *runs* this town, fool. Why don't you take your giant rat, your insect and your ragbag, and get your big, ugly green ass outta here before I lose my temper?"

Shield raised like a battering ram, Gorak charged the doorman. The hundred or so pounds of thick wood and iron smashed into the human's face, splintering the nose in a spray of blood. The impact hurled the big man off his feet and into the doors of the club as though he were a sack of feathers. Gorak followed up the assault with a violent kick that would've surely crushed the man's ribcage if it had connected. The guard, however, rolled aside with the reflexes of a cat and the troll's giant foot slammed into the door forcefully enough to tear it off its hinges and send it careening into the darkened interior of the club.

Baldy leapt to his feet, sword in hand. "You done fucked up now, troll," he snarled, blood running from his ruined nose. Behind him, a horde of guards spilled from the building's side door like hornets from a kicked hive.

Gorak grinned and wrapped his big right hand around one of the awning's support pillars. Tearing the stone column free, the troll roared, "I will crush you!" as he waded into the melee.

Feather had never seen such combat. As she dodged amongst the feet of the giants, occasionally stabbing or slashing ankles with her Needle, Gorak swept wide-eyed and screaming humans aside with his makeshift club. The troll reveled in the chaos, blocking attacks with his shield, lashing out with his feet, headbutting humans like a bull, bellowing challenges and curses, while the mage sent miniature lightning bolts flickering through the air at the guards who had appeared on the rooftop. Gorak was demolishing all comers and wrecking the façade of the building with every swing of his purloined weapon, Al was disabling archers with every wave of his hand, but Feather was terrified and nearly useless in the fight.

Suddenly, a voice rang out above the din of the melee. "What the blue *fuck* is goin' on out here?"

The guards froze instantly at the barked demand. Gorak, battle rage upon him, took the lull as an opportunity to bash a few more of them before realizing they weren't fighting back. Feather reined in Renato, and the opossum halted with his jaws around the ankle of one of the guards. Al turned to face the red-faced man with the flat-top haircut scowling at them all from The Gilded Truffle's mangled doorway.

"Mr Bricktop, sir," Baldy stuttered. "This troll tried getting by me, and his name isn't on the list. We were just—"

"Destroying the front of my bloody club?" the tomato-hued man snarled. His spotted, scarred hands were clenched in fists of rage as he glowered at his minions. "For shit's sake, what the *fuck* do I pay you idiots for?" Bricktop unnecessarily smoothed the front of his immaculately tailored suit and turned his cockatrice gaze onto the troll. "Why are you wrecking up my bloody club? Does it look like a damn bridge to you or something?"

Gorak bristled at the slur. "Contrary to what you humans believe, not all trolls inhabit the underside of bridges."

"Whatever. Don't care. Why are you here?"

"We are looking for a man named Nissan," Feather answered, cutting off Gorak's response. "A pickpocket told us you might be able to help us find him."

Bricktop shook his head. "Now I've seen everything. Sprites riding around on opossums. I don't know any twat named Nissan. If you're quite done trashing my place, kindly fuck off. And you," he snarled, skewering Baldy with a glance, "this clusterfuck is coming out of your salary."

"Nissan slew my *rasgul*," Gorak informed the human. "I will destroy him. If I discover that you are lying to us, no power in this world will protect you."

Bricktop was unmoved. "I've got a business empire to run, troll. Your quarrel and your threats don't concern me in the least."

"Please, sir," Feather began, quailing only slightly under the scrutinizing stare of the human. "Could you check to see if anyone you know is harboring Nissan? He murdered Jeremy the fishmonger in cold blood."

The old man again smoothed his suit. "Look, kid, if any of my contacts are hiding this guy, then he paid dearly for the privilege. It's bad business to renege on a deal, and rumors to the contrary, there is honor among my thieves. Sorry for your loss; truly I am. Knew him when we were just kids. Jeremy was a good man, and he always sold his fish at reasonable prices, but I can't ask my associates to turn over customers — especially not to titheads."

Gorak started toward the human, preparing to smite him with his own porch pillar. Feather flew off Renato's back and hovered in the troll's face. "Gorak, don't. You wouldn't go against your own honor, regardless of the threat. You can't expect him to violate his. We'll find another way."

The troll halted, frustrated rage contorting his face. "What other way?" he snapped. "This man rules the criminals. If he won't aid us, Nissan will escape!"

Feather spun in midair and hovered down to Bricktop's level. "Is there anything you *can* do to help us? Please?"

The crime lord sighed. "I always did have a soft spot for a pretty young lady. Suppose you were in the mood for a quiet drink and a good steak. If you happened to go to the Happy Bull, and you happened to run into a certain murdering asshole, no skin off my nose."

Chapter 25

Hester and Inigo emerged from the Cave of R'an D'om, a bandit's duffle bag stuffed with Joel's crap slung over the elf's shoulder, and came face to faces with a gigantic swarm of wasps. The swarm numbered in the millions, and each black and green wasp was easily as long as Hester's hand. The insects regarded the large mammals coldly through their red dead eyes as they hovered and buzzed about the fortress.

Beneath the swarm stood a feminine figure clad in a black and green gown which shimmered and pulsed in time with the wasps. It wasn't until Inigo's eyes adjusted to the brightness of the sunlight that he realized that her gown didn't just resemble the swarm; this woman wore the wasps instead of clothing. The elf had a truly awful feeling about this woman's inexplicable arrival.

She cocked her head with an insectile twitch, and Inigo and Hester felt cold, alien thoughts bore into their skulls with an infuriated buzz. "Give me what you've taken."

"Why should we do that?" Hester snapped, shaking off the intrusion into her brain. "You think your stupid bugs scare me?"

The wasp-clad woman smiled. "My children will destroy you if you don't. Are Joel's trinkets worth your lives?"

"No," Inigo replied. "They are most assuredly not. Have you a name, wasp queen?"

She chuckled. "Wasp queen will do, elf. It has been ages since I feasted upon one of your sweet-tasting kindred. You have led us on a merry chase since you left Joel's domicile. I applaud your use of fire to dissuade my children from pursuing you. The smoke threw us off your trail, but your failure to waver from your course allowed us to track you to this valley."

The elf shrugged. He'd had no idea the insects were observing their every move, but he wouldn't allow her to know that the blazes were unintentional. "Joel will be displeased if we simply hand over his property."

"Yes," the wasp queen buzzed. "But you will survive. Should you refuse, you will die. Choose wisely, elf."

Hester yanked the duffle from Inigo's shoulder and tossed it to the ground. Snarling, she smashed the Staff of Flameyness onto the stone floor of the fortress. The weeds poking through the gaps between the stones exploded into flames. "Or we just burn it all!" Hester shouted at the wasps. "You get nothing, you bitch!"

The wasp queen scowled at the shaman. "You will still die."

"And you still won't get a damn thing!" Hester yelled, lighting more grass on fire. "You want to get your ugly claws on Joel's stuff, go in there and get it yourself!"

Inigo cringed. He had no desire to die of hundreds of stings. "Let us not be hasty. I propose a compromise, queen. You allow us to leave, and we shall tell you how to pass through the cave's defenses."

The wasp queen smiled, revealing a mouthful of metallic blue needles. "I accept your offer, elf. What must I do to enter the cave?"

"Take the corridor to the left," Inigo told her. You will come to an enchanted door. Touch it and speak to it. Tell it that Joel sent you, and it will permit you to enter the treasure chamber."

"I will enter the cavern," the queen of the terrifying swarm stated. "My children will remain here with you. If you speak the truth, they will allow you to leave. If you lie, the remainder of your short lives will be unpleasant."

The mysterious woman and her gown of stinging insects floated into the cave. The swarm surrounded Hester and Inigo, forming a living cage of stingers. Hester pulled a length of dried meat from her pack, chomping on it in a bovine fashion. Inigo amused himself by cleaning his fingernails with a dagger.

"This should be interesting," the elf remarked, maintaining a casual demeanor despite the icy claw of fear gripping his guts. "We should probably be ready to run."

Hester snorted. "No shit. Waspy will be at the door about... now!"

Inigo grasped the handles of the duffle and slipped the dagger back into his belt as a blood-curdling shriek rang out from the cave's mouth. The wasp swarm's coordinated movements collapsed. Several of the larger ones burst into flames and dropped to the ground. Hester and Inigo dashed through a gap in their living cage and sprinted for the fortress gate. Behind them, the wasps began to attack everything in sight, including each other, as the queen's control was disrupted. Tendrils of the swarm raced after the elf and human, but their flight was jerky and hesitant, and their quarry quickly gained ground.

The adventurers never slowed until they were well away from the valley, leaving the Cave of R'an D'om far behind.

Had they lingered, they would've seen a smoking form stagger out of the cavern. Her hair and gown of wasps was burned away. The left arm ended in a charred skeletal hand. The left side of her face had melted away beneath the dragon's rage, revealing a blackened skull. The red right eye was ablaze with hate.

Remnants of her swarm buzzed around her, cooling the scalded flesh with the meager drafts from their wings. As their queen collapsed to the cold stone, they draped her naked body with a blanket of their bodies. She would avenge their treachery, but not today. It would take time for her to heal and to rebuild her swarm, but what was time to an immortal?

Chapter 26

The Happy Bull was listed in *The Adventurer's Almanac*'s previous edition as the best steakhouse in the Canabeer Territories. Our intrepid researchers highly recommend the transcendental T-bone, with the specially made steak butter. The chefs at the Happy Bull are trained at several of the most prestigious culinary academies, and they use only the finest, freshest ingredients and spices.

Along with these chops of heaven, the Happy Bull offers one of the fanciest salad bars our food critics have ever encountered. Featuring a wide selection of toppings from avocado chunks to sautéed zucchini, the Bull's bar offers up thirteen different kinds of lettuce. And if salads don't appeal to your palate, pair your steaks with eight types of potatoes, and your choice of broccoli spears, coleslaw, or beer battered onion rings.

The Happy Bull's cavernous seating area is perfect for large groups, meetings, family reunions or plotting coups. For weddings and other formal events, the Happy Bull's pavilion provides a beautiful setting, complete with well-maintained grassy knolls and picturesque goldfish pond. Reservations are highly recommended, but not required.

The steakhouse looked almost as good as it smelled, Al thought as he, Feather and Gorak stood on the street in front of the building. Smoke rolled from a lovely chimney, spilling forth the unforgettable scent of masterfully prepared steak seared over hardwood. Al's mouth was watering as they climbed the wooden ramp to the wide, inviting front doors.

A well-groomed man with silver hair greeted them warmly as they entered. "Welcome to the Happy Bull. Three in your party this afternoon?"

"Absolutely," Al replied, entranced by the scent of steaks. "Got any specials today?"

"I always recommend the Inverness strip," the older man replied graciously. "This way, gentlemen and lady."

They were led to a large table, covered in a glimmering white cloth. Gorak pushed the flimsy chair aside and settled himself on the smooth stone floor. Al flopped merrily into a surprisingly comfortable wooden chair, padded with finely tanned leather. The older man produced a booster seat for Feather and placed a bowl of water on the floor for Renato.

He pulled three sheets of parchment from thin air and placed them before the diners. "I'll give you a few moments to peruse the menus," he said. "I'll be right back with some water for your table."

The waiter vanished, reappearing at another table nearby, and Al found himself wondering if the waiter was the same type of entity as Flo. Opening his mind's eye a smidgen, Al examined the waiter. He saw only a normal human. Disappointed, he closed the eye again.

Gorak struggled to read the menu. He was somewhat fluent in speaking the language commonly used by humans and dwarves, but reading their script, with its curlicues and loops was difficult from him. Annoyed, he tossed the menu on the table and grunted, "I just want meat. I care not what they call it."

Feather studied the troll suspiciously. "Would you like me to read it to you, Gorak? I don't mind, if you need help."

The troll nodded curtly. "I will be grateful for your assistance, little warrior. I admit that the 'Common' tongue is difficult for me to decipher."

"Meh. They're all a pain in the ass to learn," Al agreed. "Totally goin' for the Inverness strip steak. Wonder if the salad bar is any good. Crap. Look who just walked through the door."

Sure enough, Nissan had strolled into the Happy Bull like he owned the place. He didn't notice Al, Feather or Gorak until his eyes had adjusted to the indoor lighting. By then, the troll was already bearing down on him like a green avalanche.

Nissan's eyes sprang wide and his jaw dropped an instant before Gorak's heavy shield slammed into his chest, propelled by nearly half a ton of furious troll. They flew out the door, landing on the ramp. Nissan somehow managed to avoid being turned into a snappily dressed paste beneath Gorak's bulk. Panicked, he rolled to his feet and jumped over the ramp's handrail.

Clutching his cracked ribs with his left hand, enchanted sword in his right, Nissan cried, "I beg you, stop! I didn't mean to kill your friend! Mercy!"

"You will come quietly, and face justice?" the troll asked.

"You can't expect someone of my breeding to stand trial for slaying a commoner by accident," Nissan protested. "I will compensate you for your loss. Name a price, and I will see you are repaid."

This was possibly the worst thing he could've said to an angry troll. Not only had he insulted the dead man by implying that his life was worth less than a supposed noble, but with his offer of the payout, he had also implied that Gorak's honor and friendship was for sale. Gorak lowered his head and charged, crashing through the handrail as if it were merely a wisp of delicious steak-grilling smoke. Splintered wood filled the air as a four-foot-long section of rail flew through the air like an ungainly javelin.

Nissan dodged aside, directing a slash at Gorak's leg. The blade penetrated the troll's leather armor, leaving a tiny cut across the hamstring. The wound stung like a scorpion sting and bled slightly but caused only superficial damage. It did, however, piss the troll off immensely.

Roaring like a housefire, Gorak ripped one of the Happy Bull's rosebushes out by the roots and proceeded to swat Nissan like a particularly large and loathsome fly.

Rose thorns ripped the rogue's skin and fine clothes, and the supple tendrils of the rose branches snaked past his defenses to cut at his perfect face. Shrieking like a woman, Nissan fell back and tried to flee. Gorak simply lobbed his impromptu weapon at the coward, knocking him to the ground in a blast of root dirt and rose petals.

Nissan lay on the street, bleeding from myriad cuts, as the troll rumbled forward. The rogue lay perfectly still, his sword gripped beneath him, waiting for the troll to close the distance. As the troll came within range, Nissan rolled over, stabbing upward with Maxima, a triumphal grin on his face.

"Die!" he bellowed, thrusting with all of his might. He felt the blade sink deeply and heard the monster grunt in pain. Nissan blinked blood from his eyes and gazed up into the troll's surprised face.

Gorak twisted his shield, grimacing at the agony as he tore the blade from Nissan's grasp. The sword's enchanted steel had driven through the ironwood, piercing the troll's forearm to the bone, but it had only grazed Gorak's unprotected ribs. As Nissan's victorious grin turned into a horrified rictus, Gorak slammed the pointed bottom of the shield into the human's chest.

Bone shattered, and the ironclad tip of the shield drove deeply into the thoracic cavity. Lungs burst, shards of sternum were shoved through the muscle of the heart, and the shield shattered the spine. The tip erupted from Nissan's back, gouging a divot in the cobblestone road beneath.

Nissan's hands flailed impotently against the killing wood. A gurgling rush of blood flooded from his thorn-torn lips. His shocked eyes stared into the merciless troll orbs. Then, the rogue's eyes glazed over, and the arms fell limply to the road. With a satisfied growl, the troll ripped the shield free. Stoically, he drew the sword from his wounded arm.

He stripped the dead man of his weapons and gold and plonked the fancy hat upon his own head. It fit decently enough.

Al and Feather had come to join the troll. Feather fussed over Gorak's minor injuries. Renato began to nibble on the dead man's hand.

Gorak looked to his companions and said, "Jeremy has been avenged. I thank you for your aid in finding this murderer."

"Any time," Al replied. "Uh, can I have his boots?"

Epilogue

Inigo and Hester arrived in Gunnar's Rest two days after Gorak had brutally slain Nissan, avenging his friend and *rasgul*. They were met at the gate by three of Gunnar's Rest's newest guards. The troll regarded them calmly, his battered shield resting on the ground beside him and his new, enchanted sword hanging from his belt.

"Welcome back to Gunnar's Rest," Gorak said. "Anything to declare?"

"They've got an entire bag of magical stuff," Feather announced, pointing at the duffel. "Pretty heavy duty enchantments, too."

"It all belongs to Joel," Inigo stated. "We have no idea what any of the spells do. May we enter the town, please?"

"I think not," Captain Phil McCracken stated. "If Joel wants his crap, he can come and get it himself." The captain seized the bag and carried it off toward the jail. "Tell that prick to consider this moment the next time he decides to screw with my guards."

The elf shook with anger. He had traveled so far, nearly been killed numerous times, only to have his cargo seized by the guards. He briefly considered slaying the captain, but only briefly. He remembered all too well the number of titheads with bows in the towers.

"I doubt Joel will be pleased by this," Inigo said coldly.

"Probably not," Al agreed. Extending a middle finger on each hand, he added, "Give him those for me."

As the outraged elf and shaman headed to rendezvous with Joel, Feather let out a sigh. "You know this isn't over, right? Joel won't let this stand."

Gorak smiled cheerfully. "I welcome his reply, little warrior."